A GALAXY TOO FAR

~~I dedicate this book to my dear three-legged friend, Barl.~~

— Harry Greene

BAH! I'M GOING TO GET YOU, HARRY YOU ALIEN FREAK, AND WHEN I DO I'M GONNA
TURN YOU INTO FARGLIAN ROACH PASTE!

— Squeaker Longstockings

ORCHARD BOOKS

First published in Great Britain in 2015
by The Watts Publishing Group
1 3 5 7 9 10 8 6 4 2
Text © Fabled Lands 2015

Courtesy of Advocate Art:
Cover artwork and internal artwork by Jamie Lenman

The moral rights of the author and illustrator have been asserted.

A CIP catalogue record for this book is available from the British Library.

ISBN 978 1 40833 030 2

Printed and bound in Great Britain by Clays Ltd, St Ives plc

The paper and board used in this book are from well-managed forests and other responsible sources.

Orchard Books, an imprint of Hachette Children's Group
Part of The Watts Publishing Group Limited

Carmelite House, 50 Victoria Embankment, London EC4Y 0DZ

An Hachette UK Company

www.hachette.co.uk
www.hachettechildrens.co.uk
www.jamiethomson.com

JAMIE THOMSON

A GALAXY TOO FAR

ORCHARD

THE STORY SO FAR

Greetings, earthlings!

If you were lucky enough to catch the extraordinary adventures of Harry Greene in The Wrong Side of the Galaxy, *then you can skip this bit. But if for some astonishing reason you haven't read it, then you can catch up on the action so far. It's actually pretty straightforward...*

Harry Greene has been abducted by aliens – on his birthday, so unfair! And after many adventures on the wrong side of the galaxy, during which he has made some alien friends and some alien enemies, he is still trying to get back to Croydon. Except that Croydon is just so far away... And his enemies are just so much nearer...

'**AAARRGH!**' screamed Harry as the giant robot picked him up in one of its enormous metal hands.

Harry stared up into the big, round, gleaming dome of its head and gawped. It looked like a huge light bulb, and it was running a glittering cone of bluish light up and down his body.

'Scanning, scanning...' grated the huge robot.

Harry was in the security section of a spaceport on a planet called Haddus Prime. He'd thought that airport security back home on Earth was bad, but this? This was something else. A giant robot thing had him in one hand, whilst pointing a massive laser gun at his head with the other, and meanwhile tiny robot spiders crawled all over him, searching for illegal stuff.

'Unknown species!' rasped the robot.

'Human, I'm a human!' spluttered Harry.

'Noted. For the record, unknown alien is a

7

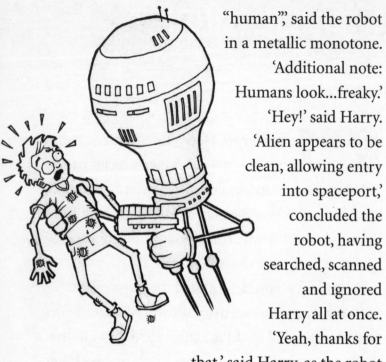

"human"', said the robot in a metallic monotone. 'Additional note: Humans look...freaky.' 'Hey!' said Harry. 'Alien appears to be clean, allowing entry into spaceport,' concluded the robot, having searched, scanned and ignored Harry all at once. 'Yeah, thanks for that,' said Harry, as the robot released him. Harry moved on, exiting the security aisle as fast as he could.

At the end of the aisle he met his friend, Barl, who'd also gone through security. Barl was seven foot tall, barrel-torsoed, heavily muscled, covered in red fur, with eyes like twin sapphires set in a vaguely cat-like face. He also had three legs – three massive legs. Two arms, though. And he thought

Harry was his mother. (It's complicated.)

Together they headed for the Arrivals checkpoint, as Harry went over the situation in his head. At some point he had to get to a planet called Volans. He knew that a certain galactic company, the Wagglestaff Corporation, were based there. This corporation published a gossip magazine called the *Supernova*. In that magazine was a column by a certain alien called Colum the Columnite Columnist from the planet Caryatid. She knew – or knew someone who knew – where Earth was. And Harry's ultimate goal was to get home to Earth, to his mother in Croydon, England, to be precise.

But first, he had to find that cheating, alien, kangaroo creature Gaggenow and his sort-of-friends, the blue-skinned cloned princesses, Alph and Bet. Gaggenow had tricked him, stolen the *Fartface Banana Nose* (a spaceship, named that because – well, it's complicated) from him (he was the rightful captain, not that alien freak, Gaggs!) and then marooned him on Tricrus. Harry had thought he'd be there forever but he'd made friends with a Tricrusian called Barl and together they'd talked the rest of the Tricrusians into giving him a spaceship to go after Gaggenow.

Gaggenow had stolen the Starheart, one of the crown jewels from the Galactic Overlord's imperial regalia, and that had caused so much trouble for everyone. The Galactic Police and a bunch of bounty hunters were after them, including one of the most famous bounty hunters in the whole galaxy, an enormous robot called Tiny Tin.

Obviously.

And that was before you even thought about the Leptira! Basically, they were giant praying mantises with spaceships and plasma rifles. They were after him too. Their leader, Clypeus – well, he hated Harry, really hated him because Harry had outwitted him.

Harry sighed. There was so much to sort out. Only then could he head for home – if he could find out where it was. And the last known location of the *Fartface Banana Nose* (he grimaced at the name – what an idiot he had been to call it that!) was here, at or near Haddus Prime. Find the *Fartface* and he would find Gaggenow and the twins.

Harry stepped up to the checkpoint. There was no one there to greet him – instead a holographic alien face appeared in midair. It reminded Harry of an old flying dinosaur, a pterosaur or a pterodactyl, with a thin, leathery bird-like head with long jaws, and a kind of slim crest above it, resting on a mass of muscle. On either side of the face, Harry could see what looked like two gigantic wheel rims.

'Welcome to Haddus Spaceport. I am the harbour master. Your craft appears to be of an unknown registration. Please tell us who you are and where you are from,' said the creature. Or rather, this is what Harry's translator said into his ear. The creature actually communicated with a series of high-pitched whistles and clicks, accompanied by a kind of sign language, using a single six-digit hand that seemed to rise up from the front of its body.

Harry blinked at it in astonishment. 'Are you a Haddusian, then?' he said.

'Yes, I am. And you're...humanoid, but not a race I recognise. Tell me more,' clicked and signed the Haddusian.

'Umm... I'm Harry, captain of this ship, the *Greene One*,' said Harry, staring at the Haddusian in fascination.

'And where is your ship from?' said the creature.

'Tricrus,' said Harry.

'Ah! We've never had a visitor from Tricrus.' The creature paused. 'Wait a minute, you're not Tricrusian, are you?'

'No, I'm a human from Earth,' said Harry.

'A human? From…what was it, dust?'

'NO! No, Earth…you know, as in… Oh, never mind,' said Harry.

'How did you get that ship, then? Don't tell me you're some kind of pirate!' said the Haddusian.

'No, no, I'm actually a Brood—'

Barl had come up behind Harry and leaned into the frame to interrupt him. 'We sent by Tricrusian Council – human is…employed by us. All is fine,' he said, and then leaned back.

'Oh, OK, fine. Are you here to refit, or will you stop and trade perhaps?' said the Haddusian.

'Well, I'd like to look around, that's for sure,' said Harry.

'This isn't a tourist resort, you know – what's it to be, refitting or trading? I need to know, so I can assign you the correct type of dock – and collect the correct fee, of course!'

Harry noticed that the creature seemed to be in some kind of hurricane or tornado. High winds appeared to be whistling all over it. Which was odd.

'Are you all right?' asked Harry. 'Is there a storm or something?'

'What? Oh, no, that's how we like it, high winds and that. Without the winds, we wouldn't be able to breathe, you see. Our world has perpetual wind, so our lungs evolved to be just holes in... Look, whatever. Trading or refit?'

'Oh, trading, then…errr…what's your name?' said Harry.

'My name.' The creature sighed resignedly. 'OK, as you asked, it's Krrlk litkikwikmik defor Milkit Dilkit wakwak mugansaul Margan-fibblenip Loobinleebinlubbin-Po the fourth. There, satisfied?'

'Riiiight,' said Harry. 'Can I call you Krrlk, or Milkit or something?'

'NO! No, you can't – shortening names is a dreadful insult here on Haddus, and you'd better remember that! Next time you might find yourself challenged to a sand duel and you wouldn't like that, oh no!'

'OK, OK, sorry, how was I supposed to know? Anyway, I can't call you by your full name, I'll never get that...'

'No, no, you won't – we realise most aliens simply don't have the brain power... Anyway, whatever, you can call me by my office title, Harbour Master. And next time, I suggest you consult your GalNav Tracker before you visit somewhere – you know, find out a bit about culture and habits and that, so you don't go around insulting people willy-nilly.'

'All right, all right, I get it! Now, what's next?' said Harry.

'OK, then,' continued the harbour master, 'there'll be a 1,500 credits docking fee. I'm assuming you don't have a Hubnet account or any Hub-registered accounts at all, so show me the money, or you aren't getting in.'

Harry held up his Galactic Credit chips.

'Fine,' said the harbour master. 'Enjoy your stay on Haddus Prime.' And the hologram winked out... And then back on again. 'Oh, and by the way, you are likely to incur further costs in the region of 2-to-4,000 Galactic Credits for refuelling, spaceport fees, taxes and so on. Goodbye!'

Harry put a hand to his chin. He only had a total of 3,000 credits. On the other hand, they had a cargo of rare metals, extracted from Tricrusian mud, including terbium, scandium and dysprosium, which the Validators back on the Mound had assured him were actually worth quite a bit. It seemed like he'd have to do some trading anyway, just to pay the fees. And he'd better check out the entry on Haddus in his GalNav.

Haddus Prime (Native name 'The Flats')

Haddus Prime is subjected to superpowerful winds that have scoured the planet flat. There are no hills or mountains. and most of it is sand.

The Haddusians

There is one dominant species that are called 'Wheelies'. They have evolved to have two large, bony wheels on either side of their bodies instead of legs. These wheels are powered by a complex set of bones and muscles that form a clever 'rack and pinion' system. But their prime mode of movement is a sail... Yes, that's right, a sail. The crest on top of their heads can open up into a large, leathery sail, that they use to catch the wind, like a sand yacht. They spend a lot of time in recreational pursuits on the surface – racing, team sports, synchronised sand surfing, and so on.

The primary export of Haddus is the much sought after spice Grerk which is sold all over the galaxy.
Be careful when dealing with Wheelies. They are quick to take offence. Their names are long and entirely incomprehensible to the rest of the galaxy..

This entry compiled by:
Verdlop Mimmlesip,
Professor of Xenothropology,
University of Fornax.

Another strange alien planet, thought Harry, as he and Barl headed for the door into the spaceport concourse. He was becoming quite the space tourist.

HARRY and Barl walked across the wide concourse of the spaceport. It was a bit like an airport back home with shops and signs and restaurants and booking offices and first class lounges and luggage depositories and so on. Everywhere people were... well, that was the big difference. They weren't 'people' as such – not human people, anyway, creature people. Everywhere stood (or squatted or flopped or folded or blobbed or dripped or... whatever) various alien beings – families, lone travellers, groups of tourists, business... Harry wanted to think 'businesspeople' but that wasn't right – business*things*, more like. And all of them were busy.

They walked on, Barl striding in front, Harry looking around in amazement at all the teeming alien life forms, half expecting to see that fish-faced kangaroo, Gaggenow, and the twins, Alph and

Bet. It was unlikely, though. His GalNav Tracker was telling him that the *Fartface* was somewhere in this area of space but not exactly where. In the meantime, Harry had to sell some of his cargo of Tricrusian mud (apparently there were plenty of businessthings who wanted to buy Tricrusian mud) so he would have enough money to be able to leave. Harry smiled to himself for a moment. That meant he was now a businessthing too!

His thoughts were distracted by a nearby conversation. What looked like a large, tentacled cauliflower, wearing green-and-blue striped pyjamas, was talking to what appeared to be a floating, many-eyed giant orange in a pink dress.

'What do you mean you haven't finished knitting my pink scarf yet? It's been three weeks!' said the giant orange.

'Have you tried knitting with these?' said the cauliflower, holding up its tentacles.

Harry stared in amazement – and slammed into Barl, who'd come to a sudden halt.

'What?' said Harry, nursing his nose.

'Barl hungry, Mum,' said Barl.

"Course you are,' said Harry. 'You're always hungry!'

Barl pointed a three-fingered hand at a nearby building. The whole thing was shaped like an enormous...well...burger. The top half formed the roof, and the bottom half the foundations. Steps

led up to the middle where the restaurant was. Outside and in, chairs and tables of various sizes and shapes were set for different types of customers.

'Galacto Burgers' said a big sign over the entrance. Harry couldn't believe it – a burger bar? In space?

'Can we have a burger please, Mum?' said Barl pleadingly.

'No,' said Harry. 'It's junk food!'

'That Astro Burgers, this Galacto Burgers!' said Barl.

'Oh, come on – Earth burgers are bad enough, but alien burgers?' said Harry.

'They organic and everything. Please, Mum, go on, they look great!' begged Barl.

Harry frowned. He had to admit the smell wafting out was delicious, and he'd mostly been eating Nutrit Porridge[1] and Tricrusian boiled-grass stew for a while now. He could really do with something new. The trouble was, these burgers – they weren't going to be beef or chicken, were they?

---

1. A kind of grey sludge made in the food replicators of the *Fartface Banana Nose*. Bland and boring, but nutritionally adequate.

'Go on, please, Mum,' wheedled Barl like a little kid, even though he towered over Harry.

Harry shook his head, still uncertain. His mum was always telling him that burgers were bad for you. Barl tugged on Harry's sleeve (almost pulling him to the ground in the process) and said again, 'Muuum, pleeeeasse!'

'Oh, all right, let's at least take a look at the menu,' said Harry. (Now he knew what his own mum felt like when they walked passed burger bars and sweet shops back home on Earth.)

Inside, a 'waitress' – in fact, a wheel-sided, bony, dinosaur-bird headed, crested Haddusian with an apron, from the middle of which extended a single arm – welcomed them.

'Greetings, hungry beings!' it whistled and clicked. 'Please, have a menu. Humanoid, reptilian, fungoid, avian or aquatic?'

'What?' said Harry.

'You know, for your menu. You look humanoid to me but it is always best to ask first, just in case.'

'Oh, I see! Yes, human, err...humanoid. Yes, thank you,' said Harry.

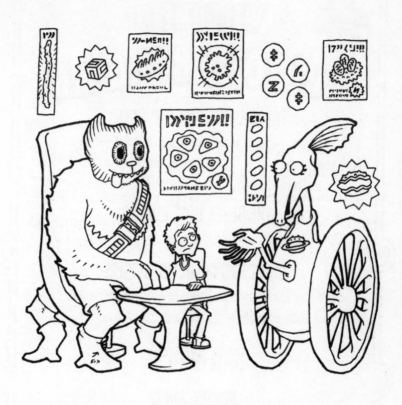

Barl and Harry took seats and looked around the restaurant. Posters of meal deals hung on the walls – some of them looked distinctly unappetising. Harry's face wrinkled up in disgust at what looked like a pile of pale, glutinous fish eggs with squirmy insides on a bed of some kind of warty seaweed.

'Don't worry,' said Barl, 'that fish food – you

WELCOME TO
GALACTO BURGERS

100% PRIME PONGO MEAT

THE CLASSIC PONGO BURGER[2]

Prime Pongo meat in a delicious seeded Grerk-spiced bun!
With your choice of savoury sauces like radioactive Farglian
roach paste, Skrench ketchup or MikMak mustard[3]

THE BLACK HOLE BURGER

Double Pongo burgers in a bowl of MikMak mustard[4]

GALACTO'S GALACTIC BURGER!

4 stacked Pongo burgers in a Grerk megabun,
with Snargle salad[5] and drizzled Skrench

·············· SIDE ORDERS ··············

BONION RINGS

Deep-fried in a Grerk batter

SPICY BUFFALO WINGS

Deep-fried wings of the Garnulian buffalo bird.
Generally recommended for parties of six or more

TOAST

The strange specialty dish that is sweeping the galaxy!
A slice of slightly charred Grerk bread, served with
Smogpus butter and some Farglian roach jam

know, aquatic. Humanoid burgers much nicer!'

'You've had them before?' asked Harry.

'Yeah, but only frozen, back home. Good to try real thing. Galacto burgers famous!' said Barl.

A bowl of a glittery, greenish-brown, sandy powder was laid out on the table. A little card said, 'Grerk, the galaxy-famous spice of Haddus, our primary export! Have a taste, it's yum-yum yummity-yum!'

'Right. Yummity-yum, hah, sure it is,' said Harry. It looked more like glittery face paint at a party for six year olds than something that went on your dinner!

Still, better give it a go, I suppose, he thought. Gingerly he put a little glitter dust on his finger and tasted it. Hey, it actually was a little yummity yum – a bit like cinnamon with a dash of liquorice

---

2. All burgers come with your choice of beetle fries, vegetable paste fries, wood chips (a favourite of omnivorous ruminants) or silicon chips

3. Warning! MikMak mustard may cause sudden explosive evacuation of the bowels

4. Emergency medical bucket provided

5. Warning! Snargle salad may attempt to escape.

or aniseed along with a peppery zing. And he was hungry. Time for a burger, maybe with a bit of Grerk! Harry looked down at his menu. *100% PRIME PONGO MEAT* it said at the top. What kind of freaky alien meat was that? Harry wrinkled his nose. He had to admit, though, the smell of a couple of Pongo burgers frying on the griddle in the middle of the restaurant was mouthwatering. But still... Pongo meat? Really?

Harry blinked at the menu again. Better avoid the MikMak mustard, then. Hmm... Classic burger, no sauces, radioactive or otherwise, and vegetable paste fries seemed to be the safest thing. Wait a minute, they had toast! According to the *Supernova* gossip magazine, it was a 'delicacy' almost certainly discovered on his home planet, Earth.

He looked up to attract the waitress's attention and he, she or it, trundled over.

'Can I take your order?' said the waitress.

'Do you know where Earth is?' asked Harry.

'What?' she said.

'Earth. Where the toast comes from? Do you know where it is?'

'There's no earth or dirt or mud or anything like that in our food, I can tell you. My, the very thought!'

'No, I mean where toast comes from, you know, where it was invented,' said Harry excitedly.

'Toast? Well, from the Hub, I guess. It's all the rage at the moment. S'pose some chef invented it or something – don't get what all the fuss is about myself, but there you go.'

'Does anyone know about Earth?' asked Harry, desperately.

'If you're saying you want a bit of sand sprinkled over your food, I'm sure we can oblige – we get all sorts of weird requests, as you can imagine,' said the waitress.

'No, I mean... Oh, forget it,' said Harry.

A memory filled his mind. His mum, making him toast in the morning before school, with butter and honey. A tear welled up in his eye. How he missed his mum! She'd be worried sick by now, she probably thought he was dead. Harry put a hand to his mouth. *Poor Mum!* If only he could get some kind of message to her, to reassure her. Just look at

him! OK, he was in a burger bar – she'd think that was typical! But it was on another planet on the other side of the galaxy, with an alien friend. And he owned a spaceship – two, in fact! She'd be so proud!

Harry looked over at Barl. He hadn't noticed Harry's tears. Barl was hungry, and nothing was going to get in the way of a meal for him.

'Barl have Black Hole, with beetle fries and side order of Buffalo Wings!' he said. 'And I won't need bucket!'

Harry gasped. 'Are you sure? That's a lot of MikMak mustard, and I...well...you know, I wouldn't want to be around you if...'

'No, don't worry, Mum, we love MikMak mustard back home!' said Barl.

'And for you, madam?' said the waitress.

'No, I'm a...' Harry paused, staring up at the leathery-skinned, sail-crested, bird-headed alien waitress with wheels, thinking about how he was going to explain that he was actually a boy, whilst also being Barl's mum.

He soon gave up on the idea.

'I'll have a Classic Burger, and some toast, but no pus butter or roach jam, please! And some vegetable paste fries – can't go wrong with that, right?' he said.

'Of course, madam, thank you!' The waitress rolled away on her wheels.

'Look,' said Barl, pointing at a thin sheet of what could best be described as 'electronic paper'. It was a copy of that gossip column magazine, the *Supernova*. Harry picked it up and they both gave it a quick read.

THE SUPERNOVA[6]

Gossip Column

01.10.4056 GMT

With Colum the Columnite Columnist from the planet Caryatid, Supernova's *favourite gossip hound, rocking it out to all the worlds!*

Poodleplums[7], everyone!

Guess what, alien freaks? This week we've got an interview with that cop-tastic, robotic galactic bounty hunter, Tiny Tin — it's all here in the supersized, supercool, superawesome Supernova!

Tiny Tin Speaks

Colum: *So, Gaggenow, your current target. What's he done?*
Tiny Tin: *Who cares? All we're interested in is the reward.*

---

6. The *Supernova* is a fully owned subsidiary of the Wagglestaff Corporation
7. A term indicating joyous acceptance of social tribute from a lesser being.

Colum: *We?*

Tiny Tin: *Err, I mean me.*

Colum: *Any ideas about where this Gaggenow might be?*

Tiny Tin: *Well, he's a master of disguise, a proper slippery fish is our Gaggenow. But it seems he's travelling with a most unusual alien — a hairy-topped, pink, flabby organism with blubbery type freako lips and little round eyes on the front of its mutoid face. From the planet Mud. Or Soil, or Dirt or similar. Calls itself 'Hairy' or 'Mary' or something weird like that.*

Colum: *Urgh, sounds disgusting!*

Tiny Tin: *Indeed. All we have to do is find that bizzaro alien and we find Gaggenow. So if anyone out there spots such a thing, do let me know, and I'll give you a share of the reward. A very small share, mind, but still.*

Colum: *You can send any information care of the Supernova: Snarfle Building, Wagglestaff House, Big Fat City, Planet Volans. Thank you, Tiny Tin, and good luck. As for you, readers — Wibnob Nabit Flabos[8], until next time, alien freaks!*

(All Worlds Copyright © Wagglestaff Corporation)

---

8. Loosely translated: 'It's been nice, but next time please don't fart all over the cupcakes.'

3 OUT OF THE FRYING PAN...

HARRY gulped. It seemed as though the whole galaxy was after him – a fourteen-year-old boy from Croydon they thought was a mutant alien freak called Hairy Mary from Dirt! Galactic Enemy Number One. What was he going to do?

Harry shook his head in despair. That Gaggenow, he'd caused him so much trouble. Nevertheless, Harry would have to fix it. And that meant he had to find Gaggenow before Tiny Tin did, and get his ship back, as well as the Starheart that Gaggs had stolen from the Galactic Overlord's imperial crown. Harry would have to try and give it back and clear his name. That was the only way to get the bounty hunters and the Galactic Police and the rest off his back. Then he could go home to his mum – if he could find Earth. His best chance for that was to talk to Colum at the *Supernova* – she'd been the first to talk about toast. Surely she knew where it came from? Anyway, now at least he had a proper address for her.

Harry raised his head. Something was off... The chatter in the restaurant had tailed away and people were staring out the window. Harry looked out – and froze in horror. Leptira – three of them, walking up to the restaurant. Everyone was scared of the Leptira. How hideous they were – huge praying mantises with horribly human-looking faces on diamond shaped insectoid heads, carrying guns and wearing high-tech clothes. Leading them was – yes, it was Clypeus himself, the High Devourer! He'd been hunting Gaggenow for the reward too, and had a run in with Harry. And Harry had annoyed him. Oh yes, annoyed him very much, and now all Clypeus wanted to do was to eat him. Slowly.

Bit by bit.

Harry hid behind his *Supernova*. He peeped out over the top, watching the Leptira. Barl followed his gaze.

'What, Mum?' he boomed.

'Shhhh!' said Harry pointing outside.

Barl frowned. 'Leptira! The ones you told me about, Mum?' he whispered.

Harry nodded furiously. What to do?

'Shall I fight them?' said Barl, forming his hands into big, sledgehammer fists.

Harry looked from Barl to the Leptira and back again.

'Two Leptira, maybe, but three? They'd cut you up bad – no, can't have that on my conscience, sorry, Barl!' said Harry.

Clypeus stopped by an outside table and leaned over the occupants – three Wheelies eating lunch. They reared back in alarm. Clypeus took something out from a pouch hanging on his frontal thorax. He held it up. It was a revolving hologram of Gaggenow.

'Have you seen this icthysupial?' Harry heard the Leptiran say through the window.

'No, never,' whistled and clicked the Wheelies.

'How about this organism?' countered Clypeus, adjusting the hologram display. Now it showed Harry himself!

One of the Wheelies leaned forward. 'Odd-looking thing,' it said. 'But no, never seen it before.'

Clypeus moved on to the next table, occupied by a pear-shaped, headless blob-like being.

'Have you seen this icthysupial?' asked Clypeus. 'No? What about this curious creature?' Once again, it was Harry in the frame.

'Never, but are you sure that's the right way up?' quivered the alien pear-thing in reply.

Harry looked around the restaurant. He had

to sneak out somehow! Clypeus and his mantis warriors stalked to another table, this one occupied by a family of four-legged, two-armed turtle-backed beings.

'Have you seen this icthysupial?' said Clypeus in his rasping, scary voice.

The turtles shook their heads.

'This?' said Clypeus.

At the sight of Harry, the turtles recoiled in horror. 'Do you mind? We're trying to eat here – that's disgusting!'

'Sorry, sorry,' rasped Clypeus.

Harry eyed up the door on the other side of the restaurant, thankful that the building was burger shaped – basically a big circle – so if he could get out that way, he'd have the whole restaurant between him and the Leptira. Also, Clypeus and the rest of them had no idea he had Barl with him. He could head for the door on the other side of the restaurant, with Barl to screen him, and once he was on the concourse, he could lose himself amidst the crowd.

'Let's get out of here, quiet as mice!' hissed Harry.

'But what about burger? And what is mice? Is it

food?' whined Barl.

'Sorry, no time, we've got to get going! Now, stand up, so I can hide behind you,' said Harry.

But then Harry froze in horror – again! An eight-foot-tall hunk of walking titanium had just entered the restaurant, some kind of blaster pistol in hand. Harry looked at the picture of Tiny Tin in the *Supernova*. Yup, it was him, the robot bounty hunter. Harry had been found!

He was about to scream, 'Run!' at the top of his voice, when Tiny Tin put the blaster down on the table, sat down, and picked up a menu. Harry couldn't believe it. What was a robot doing in a burger restaurant? The robot held up the menu to its chest. Maybe it had a scanner there or something?

Harry skulked behind Barl. He glanced out the window – one of the four-legged tortoise-creatures was jerking a fat, turtley finger at the restaurant!

Clypeus' head snapped up, and he began to pace to the entrance, gesturing at his two companions to follow.

'OK, Barl, we've got to get out of here now,' whispered Harry.

'Maybe not so good idea for Mum to visit planet where Tiny Tin and Leptira go,' said Barl sarcastically.

'Yeah, thanks for that, son. Can we just get out of here please?'

'Barl understand. You hide behind me.'

'Right,' whispered Harry. 'Let's go, and make sure I don't get spotted by Tiny Tin or the Leptira!'

'Barl not stupid!' said Barl rather too loudly.

Tiny Tin looked up. Barl and Harry froze once more. The robot looked Barl up and down, but didn't spot Harry hiding behind him. He looked away, out the window at the Leptira, whilst still holding the menu up to its chest.

'Idiot,' whispered Harry to Barl.

Barl shrugged, and began to sidle his way out, keeping Harry out of sight all the time.

'Everything all right?' said the Wheelie

waitress, rolling up to Harry.

'Go away!' hissed Harry.

'What about your order? Don't you want it any more?'

'No! I told you, just go away!' muttered Harry distractedly.

'No need to be so rude!' shouted the waitress, 'If you don't want anything, then you'd better leave, we don't like your type of alien here!'

'All right, all right, sorry,' muttered Harry.

Tiny Tin looked over again, just as Clypeus walked in, but neither of them spotted Harry, only seeming to see a large, three-legged, red-furred Tricrusian getting shouted at by a Wheelie waitress. Quickly they slipped away, Harry sighing with both exasperation and relief. They couldn't have drawn more attention if they'd tried.

At the last moment, just as Harry was leaving, he looked back, and spotted something odd – what looked like a little arm coming out of Tiny Tin's chest, pointing at the menu, but the restaurant door slammed shut before he could be sure.

Harry and Barl hurried down the restaurant

stairs – right into a group of aliens coming up the other way! These creatures were humanoid, but tall and thin like Halloween skeletons with skull-like heads and bony bodies covered in stretched, pale yellow skin. They seemed to wear only a kind of leather harness, but on their heads they wore hats – massive, huge, enormous hats braced with struts that came off their bony shoulders.

'Umbonians!' said Barl.

'Um-whatever,' said Harry, 'GET OUT OF THE WAY!' he bellowed.

'How dare you?' said the first Umbonian, its hat like an enormous wedding cake. Behind him, the second Umbonian wore what was basically a huge plate on its head. And the third Umbonian had one like a whelk, its whorls and twists rising upward like an ice cream cone.

The tall, cake-hatted Umbonian said in sonorous tones, 'I am Kallint Fumarole, an Umbonian Implicator of the 14th Cohort, a Lord High Archimandrite and Exarch of Dalmos, and you will get out of *my* way, you putrescent pink plankton!'

'Whatever, move it, cake head. Barl is coming

through!' said Harry, gesturing at Barl, who simply walked down the stairs, forcing the Umbonians to back up or get knocked down. Harry came on behind, looking back up the stairs – Clypeus and the Leptira could come out at any moment!

Harry and Barl hurried on through the mass of Umbonians who were huffing and puffing, and holding on to their hats. They got down the stairs all right, but now they were surrounded by more enormous-hatted Umbonians. Overhead, hanging down from the roof, one of several large security turrets whirred around to focus in on them with its camera – and its weapon, some kind of massive blaster... It was the spaceport security system. Harry shook his head. All this was attracting far too much attention!

'You haven't heard the last of this, you wretched little creature,' said Kallint Fumarole. 'The Umbonian Empire is not some two-bit organisation you can insult whenever you like!'

'Well, I'm sorry, but we're in a terrible hurry,' said Harry, 'so if you don't mind!'

'We do mind very much. I shall not forget your rudeness and there will be a reckoning when we conquer the galaxy!'

'Yeah, whatever, weird-hat dude,' said Harry, dismissively – it always irritated him when people started threatening him.

'Don't think you'll be let off lightly, oh no, when we take over you will be obliged to wear a hat!' raged the Umbonian.' The whole galaxy will have to wear hats, the Hats of Utter Submission, but you, you will have to wear the Hat of Crawling Worminess!' said the Umbonian. The rest of the Umbonians hooted in horror as if this was the worst thing that could ever happen to anyone.

Harry was about to burst out laughing when Clypeus emerged from the door of the restaurant, his two hench-insects right behind him. They froze at the sight of the Umbonians who in turn froze at the sight of the Leptira – Harry and Barl forgotten in an instant, just like that.

'What the...?' muttered Harry.

'Ancient enemies...' whispered Barl. 'A thousand years of hate – and wars. Bad wars!' Umbonian and Leptira stared at each other. Skeletal hands and chitinous claws hovered over holsters... The security turret slid across the roof to hang above them.

Meanwhile, Harry and Barl crept away, using the Umbonians' hats as cover.

'THEIR WILL BE NO VIOLENCE ON THE CONCOURSE,' blared the turret behind them. 'ANYONE WHO TRIES ANYTHING WILL BE BLASTED – GOT IT?'

Harry and Barl left them to it, hurrying on and out of sight.

'Phew,' said Harry, 'that was close! What's with

those hats, anyway? Abnormo or what!'

'Very important in Umbonian society, hats,' explained Barl. 'Your hat say what status you have in society. Also, what your rank and title.'

'Well, I'm just glad we made it out of there without getting spotted.'

'What about burgers, though? Barl still hungry!'

'You'll have to wait, son. We can't hang around here, we've got to get—'

Harry was interrupted mid-sentence. 'OI! HARRY GREENE, YOU MUTANT TWO-LEGGED FREAK!' screamed a high-pitched voice as loud as a Haddusian spaceport's security turret.

'Oh no, it Squeaker Longstockings!' said Barl.

4 INTO THE FIRE

SQUEAKER Longstockings was a Tricrusian like Barl – huge, with red fur and bright blue eyes. Unlike Barl, who didn't wear much beyond a loincloth and some belts and harnesses, she was dressed in purple-and-yellow polka dot stockings on each of her three legs, and a polka dot tunic over her barrel chest. Harry sighed. Squeaker hated Harry – hated him a lot, after what he'd done to her back home on Tricrus. He'd taken Barl from her, laughed at her, set fire to her stockings, humiliated her in front of her leaders, the High Council of Validators. Why was he so good at making enemies, he thought to himself.

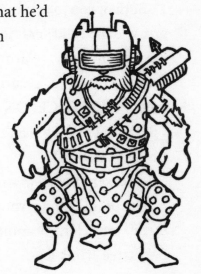

'Tracked you all the way here, and now I've got you!' said Squeaker. She grinned, and pulled out a blaster rifle. 'This time it's just you and me, you horrible little dirt-born abomination, and now you're going to pay!'

'Earth, it's Earth-born abomination,' Harry muttered, as Squeaker aimed her weapon at him.

Barl stepped in front protectively. 'Leave my mum alone,' he bellowed.

Harry looked up at Barl's hulking back. He felt a surge of affection for the giant – he was so loyal and brave!

'Both of you to pay, then? Fine by me!' Squeaker's grin widened and her finger tightened on the trigger.

Suddenly an alarm sounded across the spaceport and a security turret homed in on them. 'VIOLENCE ON THE CONCOURSE IS PROHIBITED! HOLSTER THAT WEAPON OR BE DESTROYED!'

Squeaker blinked in surprise, hesitating.

'No point killing yourself whilst killing us, is there?' said Harry leaning out from behind one of Barl's tree-trunk legs.

'HOLSTER YOUR WEAPON – YOU HAVE BEEN WARNED,' boomed the security turret.

Squeaker stared. Harry and Barl stared back. All this noise was attracting a lot of attention – again. A crowd was gathering.

Not good, thought Harry.

'NOT GOING TO SAY IT AGAIN...' bawled the turret.

Squeaker frowned in irritation. Slowly she lowered her weapon, just as a rasping voice shouted from the crowd, 'There he is!' and Clypeus and his two hench-things hurried forward.

'Well, well, what have we here, then? Little Harry Greene,' gloated Clypeus, mandibles clacking like castanets of doom. 'Tell me where Gaggenow is, and I won't eat you alive – instead I'll kill you first and put you in a pie. That's mercy, Leptiran style!'

'Stop right there, insect! That little pink blobby

thing is mine,' boomed a robotic voice. Eight feet of titanium robot shouldered it's way forward. Tiny Tin.

Harry and Barl were surrounded.

Clypeus, Squeaker Longstockings and Tiny Tin eyed each other distrustfully, hands/pincers/robotic claws hovering over weapons. Harry and Barl eyed them all – also distrustfully.

'I saw him first,' trilled Squeaker in her high-pitched voice, 'and I'm going to kill him!'

'No you're not. I want him alive for interrogation and then I'll hand him in for the reward,' grated Tiny Tin.

'I don't think so,' said Clypeus, 'because I'm going to eat him first!'

'Wait a minute, wait a minute, surely we can come to some kind of agreement without all this violence,' said Harry, stepping forward, holding his hands up. 'I mean, we're all intelligent beings, right?'

'Sure,' said Squeaker, 'you stand still whilst I blast you to kingdom come – agreed?'

Clypeus let out a series of sharp, staccato barks – Leptiran laughter. 'Good one, Tricrusian, but

I propose this agreement instead. We construct a large Grerk pastry pie, and Harry gets into it. How does that sound?'

'Turn yourself over to me, filthling,' said Tiny Tin. 'I just want a word, and then I'll hand you over to GalPol. Alive – probably.'

'Earthling, not filthling, thank you very much, and I'm not handing myself over to anyone!' said Harry.

'It's dead *or* alive, so fine by me,' said Tiny Tin, with a curiously human-like shrug.

'You have to get past me first. Barl crush insect, smash metal. And Barl beat Longstockings too!' said Barl, puffing up his chest.

'Maybe,' said Squeaker, 'but not all of us at once...'

'NOBODY KILLS, EATS OR INTERROGATES ANYONE – VIOLENCE IS FORBIDDEN,' bellowed the security turret.

There was a moment of silence. Everyone stared at each other. Harry folded his arms.

'Mexican standoff,' he said. 'So what now?'

Squeaker frowned. She flicked a glance at Clypeus. 'What if I killed him, then handed him over to you for...disposal?' she suggested.

Clypeus nodded. 'Actually, that would be acceptable – a win-win,'

'Aren't you forgetting something?' said Tiny Tin.

'What?' said Clypeus.

'Gaggenow. He's the main target, the one with the big reward,' said the robot bounty hunter.

'Hmm, good point. This is just dessert, really,' said Clypeus.

'Hey, I'm right here!' said Harry.

All three of them turned to Harry. 'Where's Gaggenow?' they shouted at once.

Harry was about to explain that he hadn't got a clue and would like to know as well, but realised at the last moment that might not be such a good idea. Instead he said, 'Seems to me the only thing keeping me alive is knowing where Gaggenow is. So I'm not going to tell you.'

Squeaker narrowed her ultramarine eyes in frustration. Clypeus clacked his mandibles. Tiny Tin stood unmoving and simply whirred. Squeaker didn't actually know Gaggenow but if he had to be found so that she could finish Harry off, so be it.

Everyone stared at each other. Harry was considering just trying to walk away. But where would he go? As soon as they left the safety of the turrets – well, all hell would break loose, unless he could get some kind of police escort or something. But he couldn't exactly call GalPol (the Galactic Police), could he – or could he? Turning himself in to GalPol – was that an answer? At least he'd be alive. But for how long? And how would he get home to his mum if he was locked up in a GalPol cell?

Squeaker, Clypeus and Tiny Tin looked at each other, and then up at the turret, their hands moving closer to their weapons. Harry realised what they were thinking – take out the turret and Harry was theirs! He gulped.

But then one of Clypeus' hench-things put an insectoid pincer up to where one of its ears might have been and started to mutter into a headset. It leaned forward to whisper something to the High Devourer.

'What?' exclaimed Clypeus, actually changing colour and flashing from a pale green to a deep purple for a second. Clypeus paused, staring at Tiny Tin and Squeaker, as if deciding whether or not to tell them something. But then suddenly, without a word, he and his hench-things scuttled away on their insect legs as fast they could go, like hurtling giant green cockroaches of death.

Everyone else jerked in surprise. Harry frowned.

Tiny Tin grated, 'Where's he off to?'

Harry noticed movement on the side of Tiny Tin's head. He could see a little glass plate, and behind it, inside the metal dome of its skull, small cogs and wheels were whirring furiously. He could even hear it. The robot was thinking, and thinking hard! Suddenly it reared up and extended its lower legs into springy curves, turned around and loped after the Leptira at extraordinary speed through the crowd...

Leaving Barl, Harry and Squeaker alone on the concourse.

'What was that all about, then?' said Harry.

'Dunno,' said Squeaker, 'but it's nice to have the field cleared, as it were. Just you and me now, muckling!'

'Earthling! It's...oh, whatever,' sighed Harry. But why had they suddenly rushed off like that, he wondered. His thoughts were interrupted by an insistent tugging on his trouser leg. Harry looked down.

'Urhgh, a giant frog!' he hollered, stepping back in horror. He hated frogs! And indeed it was, well, frog-like, and about the size of a dog. It had a holographic photo in one web-fingered hand that it checked, before looking up at Harry, and speaking.

'You gotta be Harry Greene, right, nothing else around here looks as weird as this, does it?' croaked the frog thing, waving the picture up at him.

Harry nodded. 'Yeah, that's me, the weirdo alien freak.'

Unbelievable! Here he was talking to a dog-sized frog, standing next to a couple of red-furred three-legged cat-faced giants, in an enormous room built by creatures that had wheels instead of legs and sails on their heads, and he was the alien freak!

'Got a letter for you,' said the frog.

'Really? Well, OK, then,' said Harry, holding out his hand.

The frog raised itself up on its hind legs and vomited something onto his palm, before dropping down and hopping off without a backwards glance.

Squeaker laughed out loud. Even Barl didn't seem able to help himself, and put a three-fingered hand up to his mouth to stifle a giggle. Harry had a ball of slime-covered something on his hand. He wrinkled his mouth up in disgust.

'Aren't you going to open it, then?' said Squeaker.

Gingerly, Harry opened up the little slime-covered ball. It turned out it was a bit like a *Supernova* news sheet – very thin electronic paper, like a single sheeted super-thin tablet. The message said:

Greetings, Captain Greene,
I am Werdle 412, from Canus Prime, the only survivor
of the Wheelship AG85.

Harry frowned. AG85? Oh yes, he remembered now, that was the old name of the *Fartface Banana Nose*, before he'd accidentally renamed it as...well, the *Fartface Banana Nose*. Not one of his best moments! And this was one of the Greys that had abducted him in the first place. The nice one...well, actually, the least worst.

You may remember me — Clypeus ate my arm, and was going to eat the rest of me, but you saved me. I thank you for that. And that's why I've risked my life to send you this message:

The Leptira have captured Gaggenow and the Yureshtian twins, Alph and Bet. They have them on their battle cruiser, the Mantid Raptor, *in orbit around Haddus Prime. If you are going to rescue them, you had better do it quickly. They plan to hand Gaggenow over for the reward and sell the twins once they've interrogated them. Assuming they don't just eat them, that is.*

Werdle 412

PS the Leptira are using me as an engineering maintenance slave. There is a small dorsal maintenance hatch on the Mantid Raptor. *I have unlocked it. If you can get there unseen you can sneak in.*

There was a little picture of the Leptiran ship, showing the precise location of the airlock and the route to the holding cells where Gaggenow and the

twins were imprisoned. Harry handed it t
who looked it over. Harry put a hand up to hi .....
What to do? He could just leave them to their fate
– after all, he didn't really owe them anything, after
what they'd done to him last time. And he did want
revenge on Gaggenow. Maybe this was the best way
of punishing him… But then again…Gaggenow
had left him alive, when he could have killed him.
Besides, Harry needed the Starheart, as well as
Gaggenow alive, to clear his name. And Bet had…

Harry blushed at the memory. Bet had kissed
him. Harry sighed. He simply couldn't leave them
to die. He had to rescue them. Not to mention the
fact that he wanted his ship back.

Which meant breaking them out of a Leptiran
battle cruiser…

Squeaker Longstockings narrowed her eyes
suspiciously.

'What's going on?' she said.

'We going to rescue them, then, Mum?' asked
Barl.

'Who? Rescue who?' said Squeaker.

'Well, first things first, Barl,' said Harry. 'We've

got to get off this planet, which means selling some of our cargo.' And he set off at a brisk pace for the harbour master's office.

'Yes, Mum,' said Barl, hurrying beside him.

'Don't call him Mum, it's disgusting,' said Squeaker Longstockings, who began to follow along behind.

'No need for you to come, Squeaker,' said Harry, 'especially if it's going to upset you.'

'Hah, I'm going to stick to you like glue,' said Squeaker.

Overhead, the security turret tracked all three of them.

KRRLK litkikwikmik defor Milkit Dilkit wakwak mugansaul Margan-fibblenip Loobinleebinlubbin-Po the harbour master stared at the trio of aliens before him. Two of them were Tricrusians, huge, red-furred and three-legged, one wearing weird purple-and-yellow dotted stockings, the other in a functional harness and shorts. The third was strange indeed, a small, podgy, hairy-topped pink thing, the captain, Harry Greene. From Soiled planet or something. And he wanted to sell Tricrusian mud, as quickly as possible, so he could get out of here, also as quickly as possible. Tricrusian mud was pretty valuable, and this Harry Greene seemed to attract trouble like a black hole attracts...well, pretty much everything. It'd be good to get him off the planet as soon as possible too. Never mind the fact that they all had far too many legs, and not a single wheel amongst them. They were altogether too weird for comfort.

'All right, we'll buy your mud, but we cannot pay you in credits or in Flugij-morlian-pamblobian-dikdak-wobble-flips.'

'What?' said Barl, Squeaker and Harry at once.

'Umm... Haddusian currency. Anyway, we don't allow our currency or Galactic Credits to leave the planet. They have to stay here. So we can't pay you with currency.'

'So how am I going to get paid?' said Harry, perplexed.

'In Grerk. We'll take your rare metals mud, and replace it with Grerk, a spice native to this planet. You'll be able to get good money for it elsewhere.'

'Never heard of it,' said Squeaker.

'I have, and it does taste good. But how do I know it's worth anything elsewhere in the galaxy, though?' said Harry.

The harbour master shrugged his wheels. 'Well, we'll cover all your costs, so you can keep the Galactic Credits you started with, plus a new cargo and...well, Mongo-burdles can't be Flongo-burbles[9], as the saying goes. Take it or go elsewhere. Though I have to say, no one else can

afford to take your entire
cargo, I can tell you! I
mean, Grerk's not that
easy to..."harvest", but
anyway, there you go,
it's on the table.'

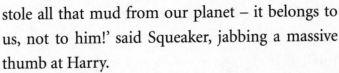

'OK, I accept,' said
Harry.

'Except he can't! This
two-legged monstrosity
stole all that mud from our planet – it belongs to
us, not to him!' said Squeaker, jabbing a massive
thumb at Harry.

'Oho,' said the harbour master. 'Disputed
ownership, eh? I love a court case, so much
money to be made— I mean legal arguments!
Legal arguments to be made, which is fascinating,
especially to us Haddusians. We love a court case.'

'Don't be ridiculous, she's obviously lying,' said

---

9. There is no direct translation of this curious Haddusian phrase. 'Beggars
can't be choosers' is the closest equivalent, but a literal translation would be:
'Poach me an egg, buttock-brain!' How such a phrase came to mean 'beggars
can't be choosers' the galactic gods only know.

Harry. 'She hates me, she's just trying to cause trouble!'

'How do we know she's lying? You've got a cargo of Tricrusian mud. She's a Tricrusian. You're not. Who am I supposed to believe, eh?' said the harbour master.

'I can vouch for cargo. It belong to Captain Greene,' said Barl.

Squeaker Longstockings glared at him. 'Traitor,' she muttered under her breath.

'It biology – what you expect me to say?' he muttered back at her.

Harry said to the harbour master, 'And our credentials on ship ownership check out, don't they? I'm the captain – it says so, look!' And he handed over his certificate.

'That's true,' said the harbour master, seeming almost disappointed. 'Well, if Barl gives me a signed deposition backing you up, that should be fine.'

'I'll sign a deposition, too – objecting!' said Squeaker.

'Fine, fine, but at the end of the day, he is Captain Greene, with a commission from the Council of Tricrus. Says he's even a citizen! Nothing I can do. You're outnumbered, sorry,' said the harbour master.

'Good,' said Harry. 'Give me the papers, I'll sign and we'll be on our way.'

'Well, unless of course you're family,' muttered the harbour master in passing, as he reached for the relevant documents.

'Actually, he my mum,' said Barl with a smile.

'Yeah, which is annoying because I'm supposed

to be Barl's mum!' squeaked Squeaker.

The harbour master paused, blinking in astonishment. He looked from face to face.

'How...?'

'It's complicated,' said Harry.

'Well, in that case... I'm sorry, but under our laws you can't be considered a reliable witness if you're related,' he said.

'What?' said Harry.

'A deposition – anyone's – won't be enough, can't be accepted, if you're related,' said the harbour master.

'But we're not actually related, it's...' spluttered Harry.

'Are you or are you not this being's mother?' said the harbour master, pointing at Barl.

'Well, sort of...' said Harry

'Technically, it is true,' interrupted Squeaker, 'but it's still an abomination.'

The harbour master looked at Barl. 'Is this being your mother?' he said.

Harry looked up at Barl, and shook his head vigorously. Barl blinked at Harry, looked over at the harbour master.

'Umm...no, no, he not my mother.' said Barl. Then he turned to Harry. 'Is that right, Mum?'

Harry raised his eyes and threw his hands in the air.

'Hah! Right, then, so you *are* related. In that case, I can't accept any depositions – we'll have to establish ownership in the usual way.'

'Usual way?'

'Court of law. Won't take more than a few months, I reckon...if you're lucky,' said the harbour master.

'But we need to get this done now,' said Harry. 'I've got people that need rescuing!'

'Looks like you're stuck then, mutant alien freak,' said a triumphant Squeaker.

'No, no, there must be some other way,' said Harry.

The harbour master raised a bony digit on its single hand. 'There is one thing... Not sure if you're going to like it, though. You could fight a sand duel – winner gets the cargo,' he said. 'This afternoon, if you like.'

'Sand duel, what's that?' said Harry.

'You get into a blow cart, and race each other. It's so windy out there on the Flats, you can get up quite a speed! Ancient sport, we've been doing it for centuries.'

'A race? That doesn't sound too bad,' said Harry, glancing over at Squeaker. She was so big and heavy, surely he'd have the advantage in a wind-powered race, he thought to himself.

Squeaker, clearly realising this, looked back, and scowled.

'Oh, it's not just a race,' went on the harbour master. 'Sure, it's first across the finishing line, but the rules...well, there's only one – you can't modify the blow cart.'

'What do you mean?' said Harry.

'To win, you've got to be the first over the line in your original, starting cart. But you can do whatever you like along the way – kill your opponent, even!'

Squeaker's scowl turned into a broad smile. 'Oh, I like the sound of that!' she said.

HARRY adjusted the goggles to keep out the raging, howling, dust-drenched winds of Haddus Prime. He was sitting in a Haddusian wind racer, or blow cart, as they called them – basically a three-wheeled land yacht. A single sail powered it, currently furled.

You sat in the main body of the cart, a bit like in a canoe, but your top half was totally exposed to the winds of Haddus. Harry was dressed in a heavy leathery coat with a thick hood. The goggles were a must, not just to protect the eyes but also for vision, as without them you couldn't see more than a few feet. The goggles read the environment around using radar, infrared and ultraviolet sensors and then translated that data into a computer-generated rendition of the landscape.

Harry looked at his controls. There was a compass, an automatic sail-raiser/furler and a kind of rudder for changing the angle of the raised sail and thus the direction of the cart. Also, a 'bolt anchor' handbrake. It literally drove a steel bolt into the ground to hold the blow cart in place. That was it.

He'd had some basic lessons but he was still a complete novice when it came to blow carting. The biggest problem was changing direction – too vigorous with the rudder and superpowerful winds could pick you up like a leaf, and throw you all over the place, and then smash you down on the ground miles away. Which was usually fatal, of course. The same was true for his opponent, though.

Harry looked over at Squeaker Longstockings. She too was wrapped up from head to foot in a kind of heavy poncho, and sitting in a blow cart about ten metres to Harry's left. It was painted in yellow and purple (of course) and she'd named it the *Die, Harry, Die!* Not very original, but to the point. It was much bigger and slower than Harry's, but also much more stable, and therefore, surprisingly, more manoeuvrable.

Squeaker waved at him jauntily. Harry frowned. He couldn't understand her confidence. Barl had worked things out on their spaceship's computers.

Harry's blow cart (which he'd called the *Greene Banana*) was lighter and much faster than Squeaker's. Barl had even worked out the optimal path for Harry to take, involving only one change of direction. Just follow that path on the compass, one light, slow turn (minimising the risk of being snatched by the wind) and Harry should cruise home at least five minutes in front of Squeaker. Harry put a hand to his chin. She must have some kind of plan...but what? As far as he could make out, he was going to shoot off faster than her and then just accelerate away. She was simply too heavy.

The headset under his hood crackled into his ears. 'Get ready, Mum,' said Barl, 'Race countdown begins...10, 9, 8...'

Harry raised the sail. It instantly ballooned with wind and the *Greene Banana* began to strain and pull mightily against the bolt anchor. At the count of zero, both his and Squeaker's bolt anchors would retract and the carts would shoot forward...

'BANG!' went the anchor and suddenly Harry was hurtling forward like a bullet from a gun! A surge of adrenalin-fuelled excitement filled him. Harry smiled.

If only his mum could see him now, racing for his life through a howling windstorm of unimaginable force on a dusty alien planet, to win a cargo of alien spice just so he could leave in his own spaceship with his loyal, three-legged warrior friend to rescue two blue-skinned princesses, trapped on a battle cruiser full of hundreds of highly advanced, deadly, man-eating alien insects who he was going to sneak past... Harry frowned. On second thoughts, maybe his mum wouldn't be so happy if she could see him now... His mate Harvey, who lived next door to Harry on Earth, would love it, though! He'd think it was just like some great big computer game in space that—

Harry's thoughts were interrupted.

'You off course! Course adjustment, two degrees to right,' crackled Barl over his headphones. 'Be careful now, Mum, don't push too hard!'

Gently, Harry pulled on the rudder control – the whole cart began to judder and shake and the right-hand wheel started to lift off the ground. Harry's heart pounded in his chest – capsizing could be fatal! Harry desperately leaned as far as he could to the right. The *Greene Banana* began to rattle – but then it

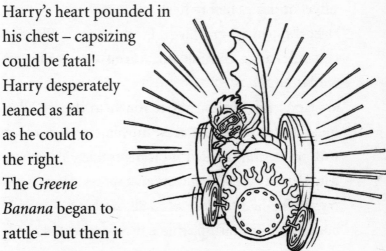

dropped back down again. He was OK.

The wind raged and screamed, driving him forward at a breakneck speed. He looked over to the left. Squeaker Longstockings was heading off at an angle, moving away from him! What was she up to?

Ah! Clever, thought Harry. She was heading on an intercept course. She'd worked out Harry's optimal path, assumed he'd use that, and was making a beeline straight for the area Harry would turn into. Good guess! But wait a minute...she had no chance at all of making that. Sure, she'd cross Harry's path – but at least ten minutes too late. It meant Harry would cross the finish line...well, something like fifteen minutes before her!

Barl's voice crackled in his ear. 'Planned course change coming up, Mum! Get ready...get ready...NOW!'

Harry moved the rudder gently to the left. Barl had worked out the precise movement required at this point, and marked it on his rudder. There was a lurch, but everything worked fine, and Harry sped on. All he had to do was...well, nothing, and he'd coast over the finishing line way before Squeaker. He looked over at his opponent, dropping off behind and to the left. Harry began to smile. It seemed like it really was going to be this easy!

But then he noticed Squeaker was doing something, rotating her barrel torso 180 degrees behind and pulling on something at the back of her cart. Harry frowned and tapped his goggles. They zoomed in on her.

There was something hanging off the rear of the cart and Squeaker was fiddling with it... Suddenly, it roared into life.

A rocket engine!

Harry's jaw dropped as the *Die, Harry, Die!* shot forward with astonishing force. What was she doing, thought Harry. That was cheating, she'd be disqualified, and he'd win by default! But then it dawned on Harry. She didn't care about winning. She only cared about killing Harry...

Harry's heart sank. It was just so unfair.

The *Die, Harry, Die!* was heading straight for him on an intercept course. She was going to ram him and his light little cart would be crushed! Harry reached for the rudder...he had to dodge, but too much pull on the rudder and he'd get smashed by the wind – too little, he'd get smashed by Squeaker.

Over the dust storm, he could hear Squeaker screaming as she approached. It was an incoherent high-pitched shriek of rage as she closed in, flames and fumes blasting from the outboard engine on the back. She must have smuggled it on board under her poncho...

It was hurtling closer and closer. Harry began to push on his rudder – slowly now, slowly! The *Greene*

Banana began to turn away... Squeaker yanked on her rudder in response, turning the *Die, Harry, Die!* back on target. She was nearly on him!

At the last minute, Harry pulled again and the *Die, Harry, Die!* roared past behind him, Squeaker screaming madly over the howling winds. But he'd pulled too hard and Harry's right hand wheel lifted off the ground... He threw his weight to the right, but it wasn't enough! Desperately, he pushed the rudder back down the other way and the right hand wheel slammed to the ground with a crash, but then the left hand wheel began to lift! Harry threw himself to the left...

He was shaking and shuddering up and down, left and right, his heart hammering in his chest, his face a mask of terror. This went on for a few seconds, but each juddering surge to the left and right was less than the last, and after a few heart-stopping seconds Harry managed to get the *Greene Banana* under control and level again.

He heaved a sigh of relief – only to spot the *Die, Harry, Die!* coming back at him from the other direction!

Harry screamed in fear. Desperately he tried to pull away. He managed to move off to the side, but Squeaker came past behind him and, reaching down a mighty arm, grabbed a wheel of the *Greene Banana* and flipped it up as if it were made of balsa wood. The wind took Harry and turned his cart over. And over, and over, and over...

The last thing Harry heard was Squeaker's triumphant laughter echoing down the wind before everything went black.

7 YUM, SPICY!

THERE she was, his mum! Smiling and crying at the same time, arms wide. He ran to her, lost himself in her mum-ish hug, the hug he'd once been so fed up with ('Mum, I'm too old for this!'), but now... now he would give away an entire solar system just for one of her hugs. And here she was.

'Mum!' he sobbed. 'It's so good to see you!'

His mum looked into his eyes. 'I'm so proud of you, Harry,' she said. 'So proud!'

But then a huge gust of wind blew up from nowhere, plucked her out of his arms like a scrap of paper and swept her away.

'Muuuuum!' screamed Harry, as his eyes flicked open.

He could hear what sounded like thousands of grains of sand rattling against his shirt...no wait, his coat – his heavy coat. And against his hood. It was hot, very hot, and there was sand in his mouth. Funny...he could smell cinnamon, or was it liquorice? He tried to look around, but he was inside what seemed to be a cloud of shrieking dust. The howling winds drowned out all other sound.

His head hurt – a lot. And his left hand ached terribly.

Harry took stock. He was stretched out on the sand. His left arm was up to its elbow in sand – wedged in some kind of hole. Where was he? The

race! Adrenalin surged within him as he remembered – Squeaker was after him. She'd tipped up his cart and...that was the last thing he remembered. How long ago was that?

He looked around. Bits of the completely wrecked *Greene Banana* lay scattered nearby and... Oh no! There was Squeaker Longstockings, trudging through the sand storm. She was stuffing something into her pockets, but at the sight of him, she hooted in triumph and began loping towards him, swinging her arms menacingly. She'd tear him to pieces. He couldn't see her face through her sand hood, but he knew she was smiling.

He had to move. Desperately, he tugged at his left arm – but it wouldn't come out, it was stuck! He pushed it forward, intending to tug it back out again, but instead he fell forward, smashing through the hole and into empty space beyond.

He was falling! 'Noooo!' he cried, but then he came to a thumping stop face down in damp sand. He'd only fallen a couple of feet. He looked around. It was pitch black but his VR goggles compensated for that, giving him a computerised view of his surroundings, as if it were full daylight. A tunnel system! And it was about his size too, several tunnels stretching away in different directions. There were strong currents of air but down here no sandstorm, and much less noise. It was almost peacefully quiet. He put a hand up to his headphones and pressed the on button.

'Barl, can you hear me?' he said. But there was nothing, not even the crackle of static.

Harry's left hand hurt a lot. He checked it – the little finger was bent at an angle. Broken. Harry stared at it... Behind him, a voice echoed down through the tunnel.

'I know you're in there!' said Squeaker, 'I'm coming for you, Harry, you mutant freak!'

Harry looked back up. The hole was only just big enough for him to get through.

Good luck with that, Squeaker, he thought to himself. But then a big, red-furred arm reached through the hole and begin to rip it apart! Harry gulped. She'd be in here at any moment.

Nothing for it... Harry grabbed his little finger and straightened it out with a yank.

'Aaargh!' he screamed at the top of his lungs.

'Oh dear, in a bit of pain, are we? I hope it isn't too bad, Harry – NOT!' said Squeaker as she pulled apart another chunk of the tunnel wall.

Quickly Harry tied his finger up to the one next to it, with thread from his tattered coat, and, grimacing in pain, crawled on. Even crawling hurt – his ribs must be bruised too, but he couldn't worry about that now. He had to find a way out of these tunnels before Squeaker got him. Once he was on the surface, he could lose her in the sandstorm. Hopefully...

It was stiflingly hot. Harry pulled back his hood to breathe, and as he rounded a corner, he came face to face with one of the inhabitants of the tunnels. Harry's heart nearly jumped into his mouth but to his relief he could see it was much smaller than him – about the size of a cat, in fact, but there the similarity ended. It was like some kind of furless monkey/mole thing with big squirrel eyes and front paws that ended in bony shovels. Its back legs ended in strange little monkey hands. It was weird-looking, but its face was kind of cute.

They stared at each other for a moment, but then the monkey-mole turned around, shoved its bottom in Harry's face and fired a jet of poo all over him, before scampering off into the darkness with a warbling cry.

Harry reared back in disgust, gagging. 'Arg! There's some of it my mouth, eurgh!' But then...the taste...it was cinnamon with a touch of liquorice. It was pretty dry, like sand, and it glittered green.

Grerk!

Why, those sneaky Wheelies! Grerk was poo. Monkey-mole poo, and they were selling it to the rest of the galaxy, pretending it was some kind of sophisticated spice!

Too much, too much, thought Harry, shaking his head. He began to laugh uncontrollably.

Behind him a voice boomed down the tunnels. 'What are you laughing at, you little monster? You think this is funny? We'll see if you're still laughing when I rip you to pieces!'

Harry got a hold of himself. He hurried on. Up ahead, another monkey-mole gave him its best shot before moving on, and then another, but he didn't mind so much now. They were covering him with money, basically.

Behind, Squeaker ploughed her way after him, ripping the tunnel system apart. Harry was looking for a tunnel that sloped up and it wasn't long before he found one, thankfully. He began to follow it upwards. He came to a loose covering of compacted sand – a makeshift hatch. Heaving it up, he crawled out onto the Flats once more. Everywhere, the wind howled and the sand blasted, rattling against his clothes. He hitched up his hood, and looked around. Nothing. He adjusted his goggles...wait, there! Squeaker's cart, the *Die, Harry, Die!* He'd come out behind it – an excellent bit of luck! Harry loped forward, grimacing. His ribs hurt even more when he ran – he must have taken quite a beating, falling out of his cart. Still, it had turned out to be lucky in the end. He'd be out of here in no time, leaving Squeaker behind in the roaring desert.

A howl of rage came down the wind to his ears. Harry looked behind – Squeaker ripped out of the sand like a whale bursting out of the sea and began to charge after him! Harry rushed on, jumped over the side of the cart and into position. It was much bigger than his cart, of course, but had the same controls.

Squeaker was pounding towards him.

Harry unfurled the sail – it billowed taut in a second and the *Die, Harry, Die!* began to rattle and shake with power and energy! Harry turned to look behind – he put his thumbs up to his ears, stuck out his tongue, and waggled his hands.

'Nah, nah, nah, nah, nah!' he sang at the thundering Longstockings. He started laughing, but actually waggling his hand really hurt his broken finger. Also...she was getting closer... And he wasn't moving...Harry frowned – the cart was surging forward, but not actually getting anywhere...what?

Squeaker was close now, really close. 'I'm going to smash you and smash you and smash you!' she shrieked.

The bolt anchor! Of course, it was fixed in place, had to be, or the cart would have blown away on its own. Desperately Harry yanked at the handbrake – but it wouldn't move, it was too big, designed for Squeaker!

She was closer, so close, almost there!

'Arrggggh!' screamed Harry as he yanked on the brake with both hands, the effort agony on his finger.

The bolt anchor snapped back into place, the blow cart surged forward. He looked behind – Squeaker had thrown herself forward, powered by all three of her massive tree-trunk legs, and one of her enormous, three-fingered hands had closed around the back edge of the cart. Harry stared into her bright blue eyes – they were filled with wild triumph!

Already, she was bringing her other arm around – she'd be able to haul herself up and into the cart with ease. And then there'd be blood...

Harry's eyes flicked down to a big red button on the back of the cart. Squeaker's eyes followed – and widened in horror. Harry slammed the button down with his hand – and the outboard rocket engine roared into life! Squeaker was bathed in a rush of flame and fumes – she gave a disconsolate squeak and was blasted away, just as the *Die*,

Harry, Die! surged forward with terrific speed. Squeaker smashed into the sand, tumbling over and over, and then she was lost in the dust.

Harry frowned. Maybe she was dead. But then again, she was wearing a heavy-duty hood and goggles. She'd probably be all right. In any case, he'd had to do it. She wouldn't hesitate when it came to killing him, would she? Still...

Well, she'd made her bed, and now she had to lie in it, even if it was made of flames and dust. Harry checked the compass. Slowly he turned the blow cart towards the finish line. He began to grin.

He'd won!

8 THE GRAVY BOAT

HARRY leaned into the mirror in his bathroom on the *Greene One* and examined his face. One eye was as black as a Goth's. On the other side of his face, a livid purple bruise spread from cheek to temple. The effort of leaning forward made him grimace – his ribs still ached every time he moved.

He reached up to apply some ointment to the bruise on the side of his head – and caught his broken finger on the basin. 'Owww!' he moaned. 'Everything hurts!' He'd taken a bit of a battering in that race, that was for sure. But the important thing was that he'd won it. And they hadn't heard or seen Squeaker Longstockings since. They'd filled up the cargo hold with Grerk (or poo, hah, hah!) and set off, and now here they were, in orbit around Haddus.

But there was no AutoDoc[10] on the *Greene One*, just a medicine cabinet designed mostly for three-legged Tricrusians. Harry had to get back onto the *Fartface Banana Nose* as soon as possible. It was far more advanced, and the computer, Dave, had re-programmed the AutoDoc for humans. It would soon patch him up! First, though, he had to sneak into a Leptiran battle cruiser, get Gaggenow, Alph, Bet and probably Werdle 412 the Grey, sneak out again, transfer to the *Fartface* and get out of here. And then... well, he'd have to worry about that when he got there. For now he was going to find out more about his next problem, the Leptira. Harry consulted his GalNav.

_____

10. An automated robotic operating theatre controlled by an AI doctor/surgeon.

Lepton (Native name, 'The Cookhouse')

Most of the surface of Lepton is covered in a vast, wet, swarming jungle. Everywhere, pretty much all the time, some weird creature is eating some other weird creature. Other races of the galaxy have called it 'The Planet That is Eating Itself' which is a good way to think about life on Lepton.

The Leptira

The dominant species at the top of the food chain are the 'Leptira', literally meaning 'Ruthless Chefs'. They are insectoid beings with four legs and two forelimbs ending in pincer-like claws with diamond-shaped heads and truly horrible gnawing mouth parts. They are obsessed with eating other beings – indeed, the entire hierarchy of their society is dependent on it. The more intelligent beings you can claim to have eaten, the higher your rank. In the Leptiran language, 'outsider' is the same as the word for 'dinner'.

Some Leptiran Ranks

Omeletteer (1-4 victims, or 'dinners', as the Leptirans say)

Outlander Slumgullion (5-9 'dinners')

Battle Chef (10 - 30 'dinners')

Face Stuffer (31-50 'dinners')

Master Stuffer (51-100 'dinners')

Gobbler-general (101- 201 'dinners')

Devourer (201-249 'dinners')

High Devourer (250+ 'dinners')

A Useful Phrase

'Snik snik rlllllllk kersh nush nush kikkik, Kak Kak!' Memorise this phrase, as accurately as you can! Its literal meaning is simple: 'STOP! I am not edible!' It's a phrase used amongst the Leptira, and has several further meanings depending on context, such as surrendering, showing you are peaceful or just begging for mercy. It might buy you a few seconds should you run into a hungry Leptiran.

This entry compiled by:

< NAME AND TITLE REDACTED FOR SECURITY PURPOSES [11] >

---

11. Best not to let the Leptirans know who I am, eh?

Harry shook his head. Wow, those Leptira were really bad-ass! He'd better learn that phrase too, though he hoped he wouldn't have to use it. Harry walked through the small crew quarters, picking up the Survivor 2000 Packhorse backpack Gaggenow had left with him when he'd marooned him on Tricrus. It had proven to be a life saver. Inside was his mobile phone, his multi-knife, and the water dispenser. His phone was dead now, the battery having run out, and he had no way of recharging it; he kept it only for sentimental reasons. The water dispenser actually made water from the air using sunlight as an energy source (well, from the right kind of air, that was), but it was of little use to him right now. The Survivor 2000 Multi-Knife was definitely worth taking, though. It was the galaxy's version of the Swiss Army knife, except a lot more advanced. It could be a torch, a motion detector, a lighter, and a sword, amongst other things, and he was going to need it if he was to sneak aboard a Leptiran battle cruiser. Harry stashed his backpack in his locker, clipped the multi-knife to his belt and headed to the bridge of the *Greene One* where Barl,

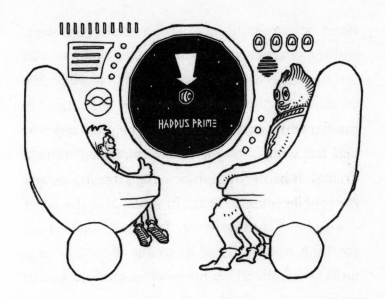

HADDUS PRIME

seated and buckled, was waiting for him. Harry strapped himself in. Some way ahead, orbiting Haddus Prime, was their target, the *Mantid Raptor*.

'Ready, Mum?' said Barl.

'Ready, son,' said Harry, and he hit the Heliobturator button. The surface of the ship began to sweat out a gel that covered the whole ship in a glutinous layer. Normally it was used for entering the heart of a sun, which was how Tricrusian ships travelled – teleporting from the inside of one sun to the inside of another. The gel would harden into a super-heat-resistant ceramic that would completely seal the *Greene One*. Nothing could get in or out – including sensors. Which meant that whilst the ceramic held, the *Greene One* should be completely undetectable, except by sight. The problem was that the ceramic really needed high temperatures to maintain its integrity, so it probably wasn't going to last for that long.

The other downside was that they couldn't see anything outside the ship so they'd had to pre-programme the ship's autopilot as carefully and as accurately as possible. The autopilot should take them to the Leptiran ship, and then come to a stop right over the dorsal airlock that the Grey, Werdle, had shown them. Once there, they should be able to dock safely and creep in without the Leptirans knowing. But if the calculation was off, just by a fraction, or the Leptirans decided to change their orbit or move or even just look out the window, they'd probably get caught and blasted out of space. Or worse – captured and eaten.

Barl and Harry exchanged looks. Harry crossed his fingers. Barl tried to do the same, but his three-fingered hands were too big and bulky, so he crossed his eyes instead. That made Harry laugh out loud, as the *Greene One* scudded invisibly through space, creeping up on the *Mantid Raptor* like a blind mosquito creeping up on a bull.

A rattling sound disturbed Harry and Barl's moment of fun. Bits of the ceramic gel were already falling off the hull. Harry held his breath.

And suddenly the *Greene One* came to halt. There was the tiniest of knocks as it docked with the Leptiran battle cruiser. Autopilot perfection!

'Well done, son!' said Harry. 'Good programming.'

'Thanks, Mum,' said Barl.

Barl and Harry headed down to the docking bay of the *Greene One*. Instruments showed that their ship was indeed docked with the dorsal airlock of the *Mantid Raptor*. Harry hit the big green button by the door, and it opened with a hiss. Ahead was the airlock door of the Leptiran ship – except it didn't look much like a door, it looked more like a cat's bottom! It began to open out like an iris, and out rushed a gust of warm and moist air that smelled of…Harry was expecting a cat's fart, but actually it smelled of…gravy. That was it. Beef gravy. It was quite a nice welcoming smell, if it wasn't for the fact that he knew the ship was full of huge, people-eating, savage insects.

The walls of the chamber beyond glowed with a dull yellowish-green phosphorescent light.

This was it. They were really going to sneak into a ship of one of the most deadly species in the galaxy! Harry knew Barl was brave…but what about himself? Was he brave? Or was he a complete idiot? Harry's knees were wobbling and his heart was pounding. A cold sweat broke out on his brow.

He certainly didn't feel brave! That meant he was... *Oh dear, best not to think about it,* thought Harry as he stepped gingerly aboard the *Mantid Raptor*.

HARRY looked around. The walls were glowing with a green and yellow light, and were ever so slightly slimy and resilient. Almost as if they were alive...

Harry checked the directions Werdle had given him.

'Down there, off to the right,' whispered Harry. Barl stepped forward.

'Wait!' hissed Harry, and he pulled out his Survivor 2000 Multi-Knife. It was a compact little matt-black, hi-tech looking cylinder, with various modes – Recon, Combat and Survival. It also responded to voice commands and had a built-in simple AI personality.

Harry thumbed the switch on its side, and whispered, 'Recon Mode,' at it.

'Yes, sir, Recon Mode,' said the knife in a voice like a US Marine. Indeed, its name was 'Sergeant'.

'Shh, not so loud, Sarge!' hissed Harry, as a beam of light clicked on from one end of the knife.

'Sorry, sir, stealth Recon it is!' whispered the multi-knife. One side of the knife squared itself off to reveal a small display. A motion detector.

'With this, we can avoid heavily populated areas,' said Harry. 'Should be useful!'

Currently the display showed one blinking red dot, right next to Harry – Barl, of course.

'Right,' said Harry, 'let's go, and remember – quiet as mice!'

Barl frowned. 'You keep saying this! What is this mice and why they quiet?'

'Because they don't want to get eaten, now shut up!' hissed Harry, as he led the way through an archway into a large space beyond. Behind them, the archway sealed itself off – so much so, that you couldn't even see that there'd been a door there, which was odd. That didn't seem right. Still, there was nothing for it, they had to go on.

According to Werdle's directions, there should be a corridor down to the holding cells at the far end of this palely glowing hall. The walls seemed to move ever so slightly in and out, as if they were breathing.

Harry and Barl moved on into the pale green glow.

All was quiet.

Suddenly, Harry's motion detector went berserk! Little red lights were flashing all over the place... Doors opened along the walls to either side and fifty or more Leptirans armed to the teeth (or rather, armed to the mandibles) leaped through into the hall.

'Arrgh!' screamed Harry, 'It's a trap!'

'Uh oh,' rumbled Barl.

A figure stepped forward from the serried ranks of pincers, mandibles, spines, spears and guns.

Clypeus, the High Devourer.

'Welcome to the *Mantid Raptor*. So nice of you to drop in,' rasped Clypeus, as smug as smug can be.

'No, no, no, no, no,' stuttered Harry under his breath, his heart filling with a terrible fear. His broken finger began to throb painfully. What they'd do to him... It didn't bear thinking about.

'How? How you know?' bellowed Barl.

Harry reckoned he knew. 'Werdle – he set us up, the little—' he began.

'The little Grey rat? Actually, no!' interrupted Clypeus, in amused and triumphant tones.

'Then how?' said Harry.

'Allow me to explain,' said Clypeus gleefully, 'with a word from our sponsor.' He held up a device and a 3D holographic face appeared in the air – Squeaker Longstockings. Clypeus pressed a button and her recorded message blared out.

'Hello, Harry and Barl. I found Werdle's letter in the wreckage of your blow cart, back on the Haddus Flats. Should have been more careful, you stupid filthling! Anyway, never look a Farglian slimebeast[12] in the mouth, as the saying goes, so I gave it to my new friend Clypeus.' So, she'd survived the race, thought Harry. Not entirely unscathed, though – he took some satisfaction in the fact that her face was heavily

_____

12. A beast from Farglia that's covered in slime. Roughly translated here as 'gift horse'

bandaged. Still, he'd been an idiot. He should have got rid of the letter, or hidden it somewhere! What had he been thinking?

'I'm sorry I can't be there, but Clypeus assures me you will be taken care of, and he'll send me a piece of the pie, hah, hah!' said Squeaker.

Harry slapped a hand up to his forehead. Like a fourteen-year-old boy from Croydon, that's how he had been thinking. A hero? How could he be hero? He was just a school kid from Earth who couldn't even pass his exams!

Squeaker went on. 'As for you, Barl, Clypeus has agreed that he will free—'

Suddenly Clypeus turned the holo device off, and Squeaker's face winked out.

'That he will freely eat you!' said Clypeus, adding his own ending to her sentence. He began to give out a series of staccato barks, his head darting back and forth like a pecking bird. The rest of the Leptira began to join in, so that the hall was filled with a lunatic chorus of short, sharp barks, like a choir of demon Chihuahuas in hell. They were laughing – all of them – at Harry and Barl.

Barl narrowed his bright blue eyes, and puffed up his chest. 'They not take us alive,' he said. Harry put a hand on his arm.

'No, no,' said Harry. 'They want me, really – maybe I can persuade them to stick to the deal they've obviously made with Squeaker. No point you dying as well.'

'Barl not let them take Mum!' he said.

The Leptira began to quieten down.

'Come on, then,' said Clypeus, 'let's go!' At his signal, several Leptira moved up to take them prisoner.

Barl balled his fists.

'No! I order you to surrender, Barl!' said Harry. At least he might be able to save him, he thought. After all, it was Harry's fault Barl was here – his fault entirely. Barl hadn't even met Alph and Bet, let alone Gaggenow – none of this was his fight.

Barl frowned. But really he didn't have much choice, there were so many Leptira. Within a few seconds Barl's hands were tied and all three of his legs were hobbled together so he could only stumble along. A tear filled Harry's eye at the sight of it. His poor friend – no, his poor son! And that made him think of his own mum. She'd never see him again. Worst of all, she'd never know what really happened to him – though, actually, that was just as well, because in all probability he was going to be killed and eaten.

They began to lead Barl away.

'Wait, where are you taking him?' cried Harry.

'There, there, Harry, my little friend,' said Clypeus walking up to him and putting a green, thorny-spined, pincer-handed arm across his shoulder. 'He's going to join the others – Gaggenow and those two clones, err, A and B.'

'Alph and Bet,' muttered Harry resentfully. 'What are you going to do with Barl?'

'We'll see! But you, Harry – you can come with

me, I've got something I want to show you!' He began to lead him away, along with two Leptiran guards.

Harry was still holding his Survivor 2000 Multi-Knife. At the moment it seemed to all appearances like a simple electric torch. But what Clypeus didn't know was that it also had a Combat Mode, and could be turned into a super-sharp hi-tech sword blade in a second. It could probably cut Clypeus' head clean off!

Harry's eyes narrowed. He may be just a school boy, out of his depth here in space, but maybe, just maybe, he could take Clypeus with him – kill him, before the others got to him. Harry's heart began to pound in his chest, as they walked along one of the ships corridors. It was suicide, really, but if he was going to be eaten anyway... It'd show them too, show them he wasn't just a useless Earth kid, but someone to be reckoned with!

But Harry couldn't quite bring himself to do it. Sure, it was a super sharp sword and he'd have the advantage of surprise. But Clypeus was still an enormous mantis thing – fast and deadly. If Harry failed...they'd take it off him for sure, and he'd have nothing. And if he succeeded? Well, he'd almost certainly die in the fight. No, it was best to wait, bide his time. For now, they thought they had him. But they were too confident, too arrogant! Harry allowed himself a little smile. He wasn't beaten yet.

Clypeus led him deeper into the ship. Machines and tubes and ducts and vents were everywhere – except they didn't quite seem like machines, they seemed like...organs. And the tubes were more like tentacles or veins.

'What's your ship made of?' asked Harry.

Clypeus looked down at him. This close it was quite unnerving. His mouth was horrible, all clacking mandibles, set in a head of pale-green insect armour. And the eyes were freaky, for they were quite human-looking – pale yellow in colour, but otherwise very similar to his own.

Clypeus clacked his mandibles. He seemed quite cheery at the moment, pleased with himself. 'No harm in telling you, I suppose,' he said. 'It's actually an organic cyborg. Half machine, half living thing. A gigantic space caterpillar, basically. Modelled on our own larval stage, when we come out of our cocoons.'

'So, your ship is basically a giant baby Leptiran, then?' said Harry.

Clypeus barked out an indulgent laugh. 'Yes, quite so!'

As they walked on, Clypeus pointed out various parts of the living ship to Harry along the way – the Plasma Torpedo rooms (big lung-like sacs that breathed in electrolysed gasses and fired out Plasma Torpedoes), the shield generator (mostly machine, but powered by chemical energy produced by what looked like enormous purple mangoes that were actually a kind of living battery), the Helicon Arcjet engine room, (large, glowing, spiky sea urchin-like spheres that pulsed and throbbed with power that fuelled the engines).

Harry had never seen anything like it, not even in all his galactic adventures.

'I have to admit,' said Harry, 'you have an amazing spaceship!'

'Thank you,' said Clypeus, even more smug and pleased than he had been before.

'How'd you find Gaggenow and the twins, anyway?' said Harry.

'Through your gBay account, of course!'

'My...my what?' said Harry, confused.

'Couldn't believe it myself – we were able to track the location and everything!' said Clypeus.

'Wha...what are you talking about?' babbled Harry.

'Doesn't really matter any more, though, does it? Here we are, dirtboy!' said Clypeus.

'Oh, for goodness sake, it's Earthboy!' said Harry.

'Whatever,' said Clypeus, ushering him into a vast room. A wash of heat came out to bathe him in moist air, laden with an array of spicy, herby smells. Complex machines – these weren't organic but were made of shiny steel and chrome and so on – lined the walls. They were tended by many Leptira, running around like gigantic ants – busy, busy, busy! They had aprons over their thoraxes and little caps on their heads.

'What the....' muttered Harry, all thoughts of weird gBay accounts forgotten.

'The kitchen!' said Clypeus proudly. 'Or, as we

like to call it, the Palace of Heavenly Dreams. Now, let me show you what we've got in store for you. The recipe is fascinating, as I'm sure you'll agree!'

Harry looked up at Clypeus and stared. For a moment, he couldn't quite believe this was actually happening – it had to be some kind of dream or nightmare, surely? Here he was inside a vast caterpillar in space, talking to a giant insect in a huge kitchen, and the insect was going to show him the recipe he'd planned for cooking and eating Harry.

Harry pinched himself, in the hope he'd wake up, and all would be well. Maybe he'd even find himself back home on Earth. But no...it was real – all too real.

Clypeus led him over to a large, round structure, a bit like a toddler's paddling pool, but made of a light greenish substance that glittered. As Harry neared, he began to see what it was.

Pie crust...

'Here we are,' said Clypeus. 'A beautifully constructed pie! Look at it – perfect, eh? Trouble is, we don't know whether to put you in whole, or

chop you up first. Perhaps even as a mince. Hmm...
choices, choices...'

Harry looked up at Clypeus, fingering his
Survivor 2000. All he had to do was shout 'Combat
Mode', and the sword would be ready. A single
slash...

'What do you think, Harry?' said Clypeus with an
insectoid chuckle.

'I think put me in there whole,' said Harry
gamely, determined not to show fear. 'It increases
the chances you'll choke on a bone!'

'Oh, very good, very good,' said Clypeus. 'You're a brave little morsel, I'll give you that!'

'The crust looks a bit sparkly and green to me – why's that?' said Harry.

'Grerk! The pastry's full of it. Add a little hot Flangle-bott sauce – yum! Grerk and Harry Pie we're thinking of calling it. It'll be a whole new dish. You should be proud!'

'You do know how they get Grerk, don't you?' said Harry.

'What do you mean?' said Clypeus.

'It's from a little creature that lives underground,' said Harry, his face beginning to broaden into a grin.

'From a creature? Like a stock made from its bones and dehydrated or something?'

'NO! It's poo – Grerk is poo!', said Harry, grinning madly now.

'Grerk is dung? You're kidding me!' said Clypeus.

'Yup, monkey-mole sand poo, I tell you!'

Clypeus narrowed his weirdly human eyes in disbelief. 'Wait a minute, you're just saying that to put me off, buy yourself a bit of time!'

'Nope, it's true, and I should know – they sprayed me with it from top to toe!' said Harry, still smiling.

Clypeus paused, uncertain. It clearly sounded convincing to him – after all, Harry could almost see him thinking, what creature wouldn't want to cover Harry in dung?

Harry nodded at him. 'It's true!'

'Oh, come on, you're lying...' Clypeus said, but more slowly this time. 'But still. We can't eat...we don't... Sprugelnobs[13], I'll have to check, just in case!' said Clypeus.

He called over a Leptiran wearing a white apron and a bright yellow cap. They moved off to the side and began to talk rapidly. Each took out little devices – they looked like holographic smartphone tablets. They began to consult them – probably looking it up on Galnet, thought Harry.

Harry glanced over at the kitchen door. There were two Leptiran guards between him and the

---

13. A Leptiran expletive, meaning something like 'blast it' or 'curses' but its literal meaning is: 'the toilet paper's been eaten by maggots, my trousers are on fire, and the casserole's exploded!'

door. Could he make a run for it? But where would he go?

Moments later, Clypeus returned. 'It's true! Those stinking Wheelies, selling us dung all this time. How vile!'

'Told you,' said Harry.

'Bah, we'll have to redesign the pie and everything!' said Clypeus angrily, his whole mood back to what Harry had come to expect from him i.e. homicidal rage.

'Oh, what a shame, I'm so sorry,' said Harry.

'Silence, you absurd, primitive mammal! In fact, take him away,' he said gesturing to the guards. 'Put him with the others and we'll eat him later!'

10 FRIENDS REUNITED? IT'S A GREY AREA.

HARRY stumbled forward into the room, having been shoved by a Leptiran guard. Behind him, the wall sealed itself up with a squelching sound.

Inside the cell were Barl, Gaggenow, and the twins Alph and Bet. Harry had found them, at last – just not in the way he'd expected. Barl had removed his bonds, and the sight of Harry seemed to perk him up no end.

'Good to see you, Mum!' said Barl.

But Gaggenow and the twins just stared at him in surprise. Gaggenow was a strange-looking creature, tall, with spindly arms and kangaroo-like legs ending in big bunny feet. His skin was a tepid white in colour, and his face looked a bit like that of a goldfish. The twins were blue-skinned and freckled, their faces framed by long, black hair (kind of like ancient Egyptian hairstyles), their eyes big and golden.

'It's good to see you too, Barl,' said Harry, with a smile. 'And also you guys, even Gaggs!' And he meant it. Well, OK, maybe not Gaggenow, but it was good to see the twins again, annoying as they could be.

Gaggenow didn't say a word. He just gave Harry a contemptuous look. Alph and Bet folded their arms, put their heads on their sides and stared silently at him, eyes big and wide, like saucers of solid gold.

'What are you'

'doing here?' they said after a second or two. The twins nearly always began and finished each other's sentences.

'I've come to rescue you,' said Harry without thinking.

'What, so you can'

'sell us on gBay again?' said the twins, with a waspish tone to their voices.

'Wha...?' began Harry.

'So, your rescue plan is to get yourself thrown into prison along with the people you're here to rescue? Good one, primitive Earth boy,' said Gaggenow dismissively.

'Hasn't quite worked out the way I planned, true – but at least I tried to save you, rather than just abandoning you, like you did to me!' said Harry angrily.

'Yes, well, needs must and all that,' muttered Gaggenow with a huff.

'Anyway, you deserved it'

'after what you did.'

'And look where it got us!' said Alph and Bet.

Harry frowned. He was missing something here.

What was...? He looked over at Gaggenow and narrowed his eyes.

'Gaggs, what did you do?' said Harry accusingly.

Gaggenow looked away shiftily.

Hah, I knew it, thought Harry to himself, *he's as guilty as...* Mind you, Gaggenow always looked away shiftily – it was his default look, really, so it didn't mean anything, necessarily.

Harry folded his arms. 'Well, this is nice, isn't it? Friends reunited and everything!' he said, and winced. Folding his arms hurt his ribs.

Suddenly a round section of the wall in the corner of the cell fell away to slap onto the floor. Out popped a little grey, turnip-shaped head. Everyone turned and stared in shock. Big black eyes on the wobbly turnip head looked around fearfully. 'Err…hello, everyone... It's me…Werdle, Werdle 412!'

'Werdle!' said Harry. 'They didn't get you, then?'

'No, though they tried. But I outwitted them. I've been hiding in the spiracles, you see,' said Werdle.

'The…what?' said Barl.

'Spiracles – breathing tubes…errr…like an organic ventilation system. Look, doesn't matter, we can't stay here. You've got to come with me, through the tubes, now!' said Werdle the Grey, in panicky but determined tones.

Harry stared for a moment – he could hardly believe they were being rescued. But then he came to his senses – if he'd learned anything it was that you had to take your chances as soon as they turned up. Never look a Farglian slimebeast in the mouth, as the saying went!

'Right,' said Harry, 'come on, everyone, let's go – follow Werdle!'

Gaggenow leaped to the fore, ever first when it came to getting away. Behind him went the twins, then Harry, and then… It was hard for Barl. He was almost too big, but with a combination of Barl forcing himself forward and Harry pulling him along, he was able to push his way through the 'spiracle vents', as Werdle had called them. As the spiracles were somehow alive, they were able to stretch and expand around Barl's body, making a Barl-shaped lump as he travelled.

They struggled on through the tube system, Harry's ribs aching all the while, his broken finger hurting every time he helped Barl along. As they forced their way through, Harry whispered to Barl, 'Do you know what gBay is?'

'No, Mum, never heard of it,' he said, between grunts. 'Ask Werdle, he a Grey, they know everything!'

They struggled on through the spiracle vents. Presently Werdle led them out of another iris door into a shadowy corridor. Everyone crawled out fairly easily, but they had to pull Barl very hard indeed – he burst out with an audible pop that echoed down the corridor into the distance. They all froze for a moment.

Nothing came to investigate.

'Where now, Werdle?' said Harry.

Werdle was about four feet tall, grey all over, his skin smooth, except for on his head, which was a bit lumpy and turnipy. He only had one arm, the other having been cut off and eaten by Clypeus.

Werdle put a shaky, long-fingered hand up to his big turnip head, looking worried.

'We have to go through there, I'm afraid,' he whispered, and pointed at a nearby door – with a long finger that was more like a jointed tentacle than the kind Harry was used to.

'And what's the problem with that?' said Harry.

'It's the Helicon Arcjet chamber. So there might be some Leptiran bioengineers working in there.'

'Helicon what?' said Gaggenow.

'The engine room, basically,' said Werdle.

'Oh no, too risky!' said Gaggenow, putting his hands over his face in the classic gesture of icthysupial fear.

'Got better idea?' whispered Barl.

'Common as muck Earth boy'

'is usually quite good'

'for this sort of thing,' said Alph and Bet.

Harry crossed his arms in irritation. But, actually, annoying though it was, they were right.

'OK, I'll deal with this,' he said, getting out his

Survivor 2000 Motion Detector. Harry crept up to the door – it opened automatically with a soft hiss. He took a few steps into the room and checked his motion detector.

No movement.

He headed back to the fugitives. 'Clear!' he hissed.

Werdle nodded, and stepped forward, leading the way. They slunk into the engine room, a vast space filled with gigantic, humming spheres that looking like nothing so much as enormous sea urchins.

'We have to sneak to the other side where we can pick up another spiracle vent,' said Werdle

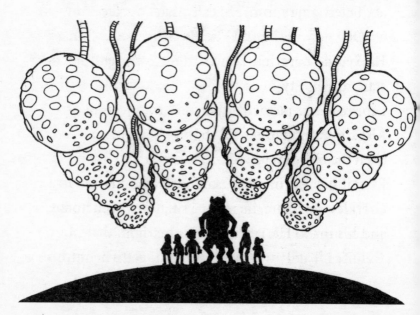

nervously. As they tiptoed along, Harry whispered to Werdle, 'Have you heard of gBay?'

Werdle looked at him in irritation. 'You want to talk about gBay? Here? Now? Really?'

'Yes, if you don't mind. What is it, for a start?' whispered Harry.

'You know, Gal-bay? For selling stuff, on Galnet, people put stuff up, other people buy it, come on, you've never heard of...' Werdle paused for a moment. 'Of course you haven't,' continued Werdle. 'You're from Earth, aren't you...? Where we...umm...'

Werdle coughed, embarrassed. The Greys had abducted Harry from Earth in the first place. It was all their fault, really, that he was here at all. Though Harry had forgiven them a long time ago. For a start, the guilty ones were all dead, thanks to the Leptira – except for Werdle, and he'd lost an arm! Also...in a strange way, Harry was kind of glad. It'd been the most exciting time he'd ever had in his life. Even if the Leptira did catch them, and put him in a Grerkless pie. Sure, he missed his mum back home, and his mate, Harvey but he didn't miss that bully Todd Scarswell and his gang. Out here? The things he'd done...the things he'd seen... Nothing could match that.

Anyway, thought Harry, they might not have gBay on earth, but they did have eBay. From the sounds of things, it was basically the same. So, somehow he had a gBay account. So someone – or something – had created one in his name. He glanced behind him. There was Gaggenow, skulking along, looking as suspicious as suspicious could be.

Harry turned back and looked around. They were about half way across the Helicon Arcjet chamber. Their footsteps, quiet as they tried to be, made little clicks on the floor as they walked. Fortunately, the throbbing hum of the sea-urchin engines mostly drowned the sound out.

'Wait a minute!' said Harry loudly

'SHHHH!' hissed everyone else.

'Sorry, sorry,' whispered Harry. 'Wait a minute, Werdle, you must know where Earth is, right – and how to get there? I mean, that's where you picked me up.'

'No, sorry, I'm an engineer. The navigators knew that, but they're dead and you reset the computer, so all the old nav logs were wiped,' Werdle whispered back.

'You've been back on the *Fartface*?' asked Harry.

'Oh yes, indeed. The Leptira put me on it straight away, after they'd captured Gaggenow and the twins. They wanted full control of the AG...err... the *Fartface*. But I couldn't get anything done. Dave wouldn't let me – he only answers to you now, so they abandoned it.' Werdle gave Harry a look. 'You have done incredibly well, you know, for a human,' he added.

Harry smiled – at last, the recognition he deserved!

Werdle continued, 'They threatened me with the usual – but there was nothing I could do. They didn't believe me, of course, thought I was Snerk ap norgle-poops findle-schooch[14], so I had to escape, hide wherever I could. That's how I ended up in the spiracle tunnels.'

---

14. Literally translated as 'feeding the hallucinogenic fungus to the Snerk' – a Snerk being a dog-like creature from Canus often used as a guard. A close translation of its meaning in English would be: 'pulling the wool over their eyes'.

'Makes sense,' said Harry. 'But what's all this stuff about gBay? Clypeus said that's how they found the *Fartface* in the first place. What's all that about?'

Just then Gaggenow came up and put a spindly arm across each of their shoulders.

'What's all this, gentlemen, whispering away? You're spooking the Royal Tsarevnas, not to mention me!'

'Hey, we're having a private conversation here!' hissed Harry in annoyance.

'Harry, Harry, Harry,' said Gaggenow. 'Let me say how sorry I am about the way things turned out, but also how pleased I am you survived! And look at you now, you've got your friend Barl—'

'Son – he's my son,' said Harry.

Gaggenow blinked in astonishment and glanced over at Barl. He gave a little gulp. 'Son? Farglian fudge! Well...anyway, umm, you've got a son now... err...and another new ship, and you're here, bigger, better, stronger than ever!'

Harry narrowed his eyes. Gaggenow was up to something!

'You should be thanking me! Really, I did you a favour, opened up all sorts of doors for you. Surely we can put the past behind us, let bygones be bygones?' said Gaggenow.

Harry shrugged off Gaggenow's arm.

'What have you done with the Starheart?' demanded Harry. 'Have the Leptira got it?'

Gaggenow gaped at him. Werdle looked over, his face a mask of panic. Mention of the Starheart always did that to people. It was the prime jewel in the Galactic Overlord's crown, after all. GalPol and all the bounty hunters and mercenaries in the galaxy were after it, including the Leptira.

'Shhh...no, they haven't, you fool. If they had, do you think I'd be alive now? I'm just glad Werdle turned up before they started the torture. For which I shall be eternally grateful, my brave Grey friend!' said Gaggenow, smiling ingratiatingly at Werdle.

'Yes, well. Here we are,' said Werdle, as they arrived at the far side of the Helicon Arcjet chamber. He reached over to push something on the wall. An iris door hissed open, revealing the spiracle vent beyond.

Harry noticed an enormous pipe running from out of the wall nearby. It fanned out into multiple pipes all connecting to each of the sea-urchin-like generators.

'Is that where all the Helicon wotsit energy goes?' he said, pointing at the pipe.

'Yes,' said Werdle, 'that's the conduit link. It keeps the generators fed with nutrients.'

Harry put a hand to his chin. 'So, if we cut that we'd disable their engines?'

'Yes!' said Werdle. 'If you managed that, they'd

have to regrow one – it'd take some time, give us the chance to get well and truly away from them!'

'Good,' said Harry, and then: 'Combat Mode!'

Immediately, a wickedly sharp, black-matt sword blade snapped out from the end of his Survivor 2000 Multi-Knife. Gaggenow hopped back with a fearful squeak, which made Harry smile. He walked over to the conduit and slashed at it. The sword cut through it like a hot knife through Smogpus butter, and in moments he'd severed it completely.

The sea urchins began to deflate, their spines slowly sinking to the ground, and the humming sound began to die off.

'Brilliant! We'd better go – now. There'll be Leptiran engineers swarming all over the place in a few seconds,' said Werdle, ushering everyone into the spiracle vents.

HARRY, Barl, Gaggenow, Werdle and the twins hurried on, squeezing their way through the vents. Suddenly they froze, scared into immobility. They could hear voices.

Leptirans!

'Pinchnip, look. That's odd,' said one voice.

'What is it, Goreus?' responded another.

'Up there, look. See that spiracle vent running along the ceiling?' said Goreus.

'Yeah... Oh yeah, what's that weird lump? Looks like a blockage,' said Pinchnip.

Harry put a panicked hand up to his head. Barl was that weird lump! What to do?

'Can't have blockages in the vent system! We'll have to cut it down, clear it out, stitch it back up,' said Goreus.

Harry thought furiously, but there was no time!

131

'Right. Here are the secateurs, there you go... Reach up...bit more, bit more...there!'

Twin scissor blades ripped into the vent, right between Harry and Barl, and began to cut. Barl and Harry tried to back away, but there was no time. Snicker-snack, and the vent was cut in two, the tubes flopping down. Unable to stop themselves, they fell through, tumbling onto the floor. Out came Barl and Harry and Gaggenow and the twins, all landing in a heap on the ground. Werdle managed to grab the torn edge of the vent and clung on with his one arm, dangling in mid-air.

'It's the prisoners, they've escaped!' screamed a startled, thin-looking Leptiran with brown markings on his carapace – Pinchnip, judging by his voice.

'Get 'em!' screamed Goreus, a shorter, but heavier-set Leptiran, with a brown chevron on his forehead.[15] Goreus leaped forward, mandibles and pincers clacking!

---

15. Brown markings painted on the exoskeleton of the Leptira marked them as bioengineers responsible for maintaining the giant Leptiran caterpillar battle cruisers.

Goreus was straddling a fallen Barl, about to snip off a leg, and Pinchnip had one of the twins under a clawed foot, about to slash down, when Harry, recalling the phrase he had memorised from the GalNav shouted, 'Snik snik rlllllllk kersh nush nush kikkik, Kak Kak!'[16]

The Leptirans couldn't help themselves and they froze for a second or two, long enough for Barl to surge up and smash Goreus down with both his fists, crushing him like a bug.

'Combat Mode, Sergeant!' screamed Harry, and he swung his sword at Pinchnip. But his ankle suddenly gave way with an agonising wrench as he stepped forward to swing – he'd obviously turned it

---

16. As you will recall, this is Leptiran for: 'Stop, I am not edible!'

when he fell out of the vent, the initial pain having been masked by adrenalin. His sword cut went astray. Pinchnip turned on Harry, screeched at him, and grabbed his shoulder.

With his pincers.

Harry yelped in agony as the pincer cut into his upper arm. Reflexively, he slashed back at the Leptiran with his sword – and neatly cut off Pinchnip's head.

And that was that.

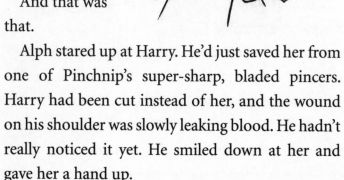

Alph stared up at Harry. He'd just saved her from one of Pinchnip's super-sharp, bladed pincers. Harry had been cut instead of her, and the wound on his shoulder was slowly leaking blood. He hadn't really noticed it yet. He smiled down at her and gave her a hand up.

'Thank you, Harry,' said Alph, her eyes wide and glistening like liquid gold, staring at his bleeding arm.

'Yes,' said Bet, 'thank you.'

Harry nodded. Suddenly his arm began to sting painfully. He pressed the cut with one hand. He could hardly believe it! He'd just been in a swordfight with an alien.

'Yes, just what one would expect from a primitive,' said Gaggenow. 'Neanderthal violence and blind aggression...'

Harry turned and narrowed his eyes, pointing his sword at Gaggenow.

Gaggenow paled, and added, 'Which can be useful at times, of course. Very useful!'

'When you've finished having a bit of a chat, can someone please get me down?' snapped an exasperated Werdle, who was still clinging to the severed lip of the spiracle vent.

Barl nodded, stepped over and gently lifted Werdle back to the ground, then, reaching into a belt pouch, he took out a padded bandage, and applied it to Harry's arm wound.

'Thanks, Barl,' said Harry as he looked around. 'This is where we first arrived, isn't it? There should be a door at the far end that leads to the airlock!' said Harry.

'Correct,' said Werdle, 'let's go.'

They headed down the hall. A sound behind them made them pause. Looking behind...

No, it couldn't be!

Goreus had recovered, and although his carapace was dented and oozing some kind of pale yellow ichor, he was up on his feet! He'd limped over to Pinchnip, and picked up his head.

And now he was fixing it back on...

The sound they'd heard was his head clicking back into place! With a thrill of horror, Harry could see Pinchnip getting up too. A cockroach's head and body could live on separately after decapitation – but this? Wow, the Leptira were really, really, really bad-ass!

'Run!' said Gaggenow and he loped off to the far end. Gaggenow's preferred strategy was always to make a run for it, and this time he was probably right, thought Harry. He turned to follow, but all he could do was limp along on his twisted ankle. Suddenly Barl swept him up into his powerful arms and ran on, carrying him.

'I got you, Mum,' he said.

Harry relaxed into his mighty arms. Barl's red fur smelled of curry which reminded Harry of home.

They reached the far door, and risked a look behind. The Leptira were moving towards them, albeit slowly. Goreus, dented and bashed, was holding something up to where his ears might be.

And an alarm started braying throughout the ship, a high-pitched shrieking sound.

'Quick, they'll be here soon,' hollered Werdle. 'Into the airlock, everyone!'

They bundled in – ahead was the entrance to the *Greene One*. They were almost there! Barl put Harry down and leaped forward, turning the wheel handle of the lock as fast as he could. Behind them, they could hear the thrumming patter of many insectoid feet.

The door swung open and they dived in.

'Shut it behind you!' said Harry. 'Me and Barl

have to get to the bridge!'

Barl swept him up and they rushed away. Gaggenow, of course, came on close behind, leaving Werdle and the twins to turn the massive wheel handle, designed as it was for huge Tricrusians.

Typical, thought Harry, but he could see that the twins and the Grey were getting the job done – just in time as now they could hear the Leptira hammering on the airlock door...

Meanwhile, Barl raced up to the bridge, dropped Harry into the captain's chair, and leaped into his own. They strapped themselves in, which hurt Harry's ribs, ankle, hand and wounded arm, but he barely noticed.

'Disengaging docking collar,' said Barl.

'Ionising xenon gas!' said Harry.

Moments later, everyone else rushed in.

'Strap yourselves in!' said Harry.

'There's only one other chair!' said Werdle.

'I'll take that,' said Gaggenow, and he jumped into it. The others grabbed on to the back of the chairs as best they could.

'Ion drive on!' said Harry, pressing the button

on his joystick control. Slowly the *Greene One* began to ease away into space, gathering speed. They'd made it!

But then the communications monitor crackled into life above their heads.

Clypeus' face appeared.

'Very resourceful, Harry, but we've got you on our sensors now, and you're crawling along! Let's see...hah, an ion drive? Our arcjet engines are faster than yours by a factor of twenty!'

'We'll see,' said Harry grimly, pushing the button on his joystick as hard as he could, willing his ship onwards.

'And don't think you can try to hide again like you did last time – we've got you on visual now!' said Clypeus.

'Face it, Clypeus, you're never going to get me in one of your pies. Never! We sneaked in, rescued our people right from under your little insect noses, and got out again. We beat you fair and square!'

'What?' screamed Clypeus. 'You think you can beat us? Why, you little primitive ape, you barely evolved cave dweller, you're no better than a Fibble-bloater!'[17]

Harry just grinned.

'We're going to get you, and this time we're going to eat you alive! Activate arcjet engines, and pursue!' shrieked Clypeus.

Harry's grin grew even bigger.

'What?' said Clypeus as a Leptiran engineer leaned into view. He said something to Clypeus.

Harry pushed on the joystick – with every second that passed they were getting further and further away.

'What do you mean? What's wrong with them?' said Clypeus, his mandibles clacking insanely and his pincers twitching with anger.

'I sabotaged them, Clypeus,' said Harry. 'See you later, alligator!'

'Noooooo, not again!' was the last thing Harry heard Clypeus say before the *Greene One* accelerated away out of range of the Leptiran sensors and, more

---

17. A type of small marsupial shrew native to the planet Lepton and famous for its bloating flatulence defence mechanism.

importantly, its weapon systems.

Harry sat back in his chair. 'Werdle, where's the *Fartface Banana Nose*?' he said.

'Hiding inside an asteroid cluster. Here, I'll programme it into your autopilot. We can be there in minutes, Captain,' said Werdle.

Harry leaned his head back. He had a bruise on his head, a broken finger and a cracked rib from when his blow cart had been destroyed in a duel to the death in a howling sandstorm on a hot, dusty, desert planet. His ankle ached terribly, from when he'd twisted it after he'd been cut out of the ventilation system on the inside of a gigantic living caterpillar in space. His T-shirt was soaked with blood from the cut he'd taken on his arm in hand-to-hand combat with a gigantic alien praying mantis that was trying to capture him, so its boss could eat him.

Typical day, really, for Captain Harry Greene, he thought. And then he passed out.

'**NO,** you can't have a burger!' said Mum, as they walked through Croydon shopping centre on a busy Saturday morning.

'Not that kind of burger, Mum. These are healthy burgers – organic and everything!' said Harry.

'Really, Harry? Who makes them, then?' said his mother.

'Well, they're Pongo burgers from the planet Pong, in a special bun, spiced up with alien poo and...'

Mum pulled up short, turned towards him, put her hands on her hips and gave him 'the look'.

'Ah...umm...fruit salad, then?' said Harry.

Harry woke with a start...

And screamed! Hovering over him was a huge robotic eye, on the end of long, articulated, gleaming white mechanical arm. Several other machine arms ended in little scalpels and saws and knives and needles...

'It's all right, Harry, it's just the AutoDoc!' said a voice.

'Dave, is that you?' said Harry.

'Yes, Captain, it's me,' said Dave. 'Welcome back. I must say, I have missed you. Well, sort of. Being a computer and that...'

'Well, I missed you,' said Harry, sitting up, 'that's for sure!'

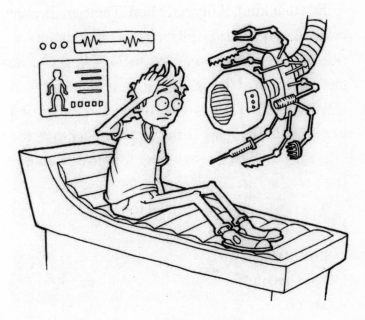

'Glad to hear it, Captain,' said Dave.

Harry looked around. He was in the med bay, lying

on a bed. (A bed designed for Greys, though, so his feet stuck out over the end.) The white gleaming thing with an eye and the knives and the needles and the rest were indeed the AutoDoc. Of course!

'How am I doing?' said Harry.

'The AutoDoc has patched you up nicely. Your bruises have been drained, and your wound sealed with Bioglue – watch out, though, it will be a bit stiff for a while. The tendons and ligaments of your ankle have been de-swollen and recalibrated, your ribcage reset and the bones in your little finger – well they were so bad it was easier to remove it and then regenerate it. Don't worry, though, regeneration usually ends up being better and stronger than the original and with Grey cloning technology, always 100 per cent successful.'

Harry held up his left hand to take a look at his finger.

'Errr...Dave?'

'Yes, Captain?'

'My finger...it's...'

The little finger had indeed been regenerated...

Into the finger of a Grey! It was long, and thin,

with an extra joint in it –
more like a bony tentacle
than a human digit.

'Oh dear,' said Dave.

'I thought you'd reset
the AutoDoc for humans!'

'Well...humanoids,
certainly,' said Dave.

'Fix it, Dave, fix it!
I can't go round with a squid-finger, it's hideous!'
wailed Harry.

'Yes...of course. I'll...run some diagnostics, try to
recalibrate the DNA settings,'

'How long will that take?'

'I...I don't know, I'm afraid, Harry,' said Dave.

Harry held up his finger. It felt...weird. He
waggled it. It waggled well enough, but like a squid's
tentacle, all wavy and horrible.

Great, that's just great, thought Harry to himself.
He put his head back on the pillow and sighed.

'How's the ship?' he said.

'In reasonable condition, I must say – I've
allowed Werdle to do some basic maintenance, and

it's looking good. Well, considering what it's been through. Running at about ninety per cent but still needs some work. There's that hole in the hull of the cargo hold, for instance, from the collision with that passenger cruise ship, the SS *Bliss*, way back when.'

'That force field thingy still in place?' said Harry.

'The Hermetic Force Bubble? Yes, and still draining energy from the Fusion Banks. Recommend purchase of fusion cells at next port of call, and full hull repairs.'

'Right. And how long have I been out?' said Harry.

'A day.'

Harry sat up with a start. 'A whole day? What about the Leptira? They know where we are, don't they?'

'Yes, yes, but don't worry, Werdle assures me it'll be at least two more days before they can get their engines back on line.'

Harry sank back again. 'Thank the stars for that!'

'You have visitors, Harry. Shall I show them in?' said Dave.

'Oh! Yeah, right, of course,' said Harry, slipping his squid-fingered left hand under the sheets.

The twins Alph and Bet, Werdle and Barl all filed into the room. No Gaggenow, though... Mind you, that was hardly surprising.

'Hi, guys,' said Harry, waving a stiff greeting. The cut on his right arm was still a bit painful, and it hurt to lift it, so he'd almost used his left hand for a moment there...

'You feeling better now, Mum?' said Barl.

'Yeah, thanks, Barl,' said Harry.

'Glad to hear it,' said Werdle. 'You did good back there!'

Harry nodded his thanks. He looked at the twins expectantly. But they just folded their arms and stared at him with their big eyes, like golden suns in a bright blue summer sky.

'I'm feeling very tired, though,' said Harry, still staring back at the twins.

'You need another twelve hours' rest or so,' said Dave.

'Not sure if we can hang around here for that long – we need to get going,' said Harry.

'Quite so,' said Werdle, 'but we can deal with that. I can set the Quantum Interstitial Drive. Jump to another star – if you give the orders, of course. Dave won't listen to anyone but you.'

'Right. Thanks, Werdle, you're a really good man – for a Grey,' said Harry with a smile.

'What makes you think I'm male?' said Werdle.

Barl, Harry and the twins all turned to stare in surprise.

'Wha...?' stuttered Harry.

'I'm female, you idiot! All of us are,' said Werdle.

'All the Greys are female?' echoed a stupefied Harry.

'Indeed,' said Werdle.

'But then...how do you...well, you know?' said Harry.

'We don't! With our cloning technology we just clone ourselves, according to what we need – scientists, leaders, engineers, and so on,' said Werdle.

Harry's jaw dropped. 'But what about the men?'

'Oh, we're much better off without them. Smelly, dirty things. Fighting all the time. And really, not so bright. Who needs 'em?' said Werdle.

'Hah, that sounds'

'about right!' said the twins, who grinned at Harry triumphantly.

Harry rolled his eyes.

'Yeah, thanks, girls. But you wouldn't have got very far without me, right? Without this boy, right here! Me!' said Harry, putting his hand up in the air.

His left hand...with the squid finger.

'Ewwwww, look at'

'the mutant Earthboy!' said the twins.

They started to screech like cats, which was how they laughed – scornfully of course.

Werdle put a squid-fingered hand up to her mouth and begin to shake with laughter too – in her case, it was a kind of warbling musical sound. Even Barl had to stifle a giggle.

Harry sighed and folded his arms glumly.

'Sorry, sorry,' said Werdle. 'AutoDoc error? Don't worry, I'm sure the computer...err...Dave, I mean... can fix it. And you're right, Harry, we wouldn't have made it without you, it's true.'

'Thanks, Werdle,' said Harry, brightening up a bit.

'I was going to add that you're nothing like a Grey male would be, of course, but actually...' And she pointed at his hand.

She and the twins started laughing again.

'Hah, hah,' said Harry. 'I wonder how you'd feel if it happened to you, eh?'

'Well, I'd pull my finger out and get it fixed,' said Alph, which caused them all to collapse into laughter again.

'Why'd you abandon me on that planet, Bet?' said Harry.

That stopped the laughter, much to Harry's satisfaction.

There's was a moment's pause. And then:

'Because you tried'

'to sell us on gBay,' said the twins.

'That's ridiculous! How could you even think that? Gaggenow just told you that, didn't he? And you just believed him? You believed him, over me, after all I've done for you!'

'No, he showed us,' said Bet.

'Oh, come on, don't give me that!' said Harry.

'Want proof? Dave, bring up Galnet gBay page, account holder Harry Greene,' said Alph.

'Shall I, Harry?' said Dave.

'Yeah, do it, this should be interesting!' said Harry.

A holographic monitor appeared in the air, with

the Galnet (Galactic Internet) search page up. Dave navigated to gBay and brought up the relevant page.

gBAY

FOR SALE: Royal Yureshtian Tsarevnas, the twins Alph and Bet[18]

ITEM CONDITION: Mostly good, almost new, a little cantankerous[19]

DELIVERY: Buyer pick-up only

QUANTITY: 2

RETURNS: No Way!

STARTING BID: 100,000 Galactic Credits

SELLER INFORMATION: Captain_Harry_Greene

CONTACT: HarryGreene@Primitive_Earth_Boy.co.gal

0% Positive Feedback (first sale)

BIDS: One bid uploaded (visual)

---

18. True names are secret until official royal investiture day.
19. Some might say very cantankerous.

'What the...?' muttered Harry, incredulous.

'Don't tell us'

'this isn't you,' said the twins.

'It isn't me!' said Harry. 'It's identity theft, I tell you!'

'Yeah'

'right,' said the twins.

'If Mum say it fake, then it fake!' said Barl.

'Well, you would'

'say that, wouldn't you?' said the twins.

Werdle put a squid-fingered hand up to her chin. 'Computer...what's that link there, the visual bid?' she said.

'Uploaded video negotiation,' said Dave.

'Can we see it?' said Werdle.

'Sure – shall I display the video, Captain?' said Dave.

'Yup, do it, Dave!' said Harry, and the monitor began to play.

At first, all that came up was a rotating buffering symbol. Harry crossed his arms and sighed. Broadband out here on the edge of the galaxy was pretty poor. He frowned. Something felt odd... He looked down. Where he'd folded his arms, he noticed that his squid finger was dangling down and tickling his side.

'Urggh!' he muttered before hiding it under the bed clothes once more.

The video started. Harry's jaw dropped in amazement. It was the face of a Leptiran, except painted blue, with freckles and with large fake gold contact lenses where its eyes should have been. And it was wearing a wig. Clearly it was a Leptiran clumsily trying to disguise itself as a blue-skinned, golden-eyed Yureshtian!

The twins began to laugh.

'How absurd!' they said together.

'Greetings, I am...errr... Yuresh. Of Yureshto. We're interested in getting our Tsarevnas back, and are happy to pay the price,' said the Leptiran.

'100,000 credits?' said a voice.

'I know that voice, it's—' said Harry.

'100,000, yes, no problem. Where do we go for

pick-up?' continued the Leptiran.

'Excellent! As for pick-up, transfer the money to my account first, then I'll drop them off at a convenient place,' said the voice

'GAGGENOW!' said Harry. Of course it was – Harry had sort of known that already.

'Well, duh! Gaggenow told us'

'that you'd disguised'

'your voice to sound like his,' said the twins.

'Oh, come on!' said Harry.

The video continued.

'How do we know we can trust you?' said the fake Yureshtian.

'Well, you'll just have to take that chance,' said Gaggenow, 'if you want the princesses back.'

'Actually...no need... There!' said the disguised Leptiran. 'We have traced your Galnet IP with our Comms Tracer App. We've found you – ah, you're just round the corner, how convenient!'

'Aiieeee!' cried the voice, and the video went dead as the link was cut.

'And that's how they found'

'where we were'

'and came for us!' said the twins.

'Look, it wasn't me! I wouldn't be so stupid as to fall for that disguise, for a start,' said Harry.

'But you might not'

'care who you offloaded us on to'

'as long as you got your credits!' said the twins.

'No, that's Gaggenow, not me! Why won't you believe me?' said Harry.

'Wait a second,' said Werdle. 'Dave, isn't there a ship's webcam on the Galnet comms station?'

'Yes, I've checked that. It was disabled for the external broadcast – so it was voice only,' said Dave.

'Except,' said Werdle,' that it might still have been on, but not transmitting externally, right?'

'Oh, yes, that's possible. Very clever, Werdle. Let's see...yes! Here we are, we can see our mysterious seller now...'

The screen began buffering. Everyone stared expectantly.

And there he was! Gaggenow himself, fish face and all.

'I knew it!' said Harry.

The twins gaped up at the monitor.

Harry turned to them. 'Well, I think you owe me an apology,' he said.

They just blinked at him.

'Well?'

'I guess we do,' said Alph with a flicker of irritation.

Bet put a hand up to her mouth and uttered a choked gasp. 'And we marooned you on that planet too!'

Alph looked at the floor shiftily, while Bet hurried forward.

'I'm so sorry, Harry!' she said.

She looked really quite distressed, thought Harry. And then...she hugged him!.

'Umm...that's OK, Bet, I forgive you...' he said without thinking, and hugged her back. As he did so, he noticed his little squid finger trailing around her shoulder. Arg!

She stepped back. 'Alph too?'

'Yes, even Alph,' said Harry grinning over at her. She smiled tentatively back at him.

'I'm sorry, Harry,' she said. 'Gaggenow lied to us the whole time!'

'Yup, right from the start,' said Harry, smiling from ear to ear. It explained a lot, in fact.

'We've been idiots,' said Bet.

'To be fair to ourselves, he is as common as muck, and from a primitive planet, so it's hardly surprising we found it difficult to believe his side of things, is it?' said Alph.

Bet looked a bit embarrassed.

'Riiight,' said Harry. 'And I suppose me coming back and rescuing you from a Leptiran battle cruiser – that was just my job because I am a commoner and I'm supposed to do that sort of thing for my... let's see...my betters? Is that it?'

'Something like that,' said Alph, unable to meet Harry's eyes.

Harry threw his hands up in disgust – and then

wished he hadn't as his little finger wobbled like jelly through the air.

'Anyway,' said Werdle, trying to diffuse the situation, 'what are we going to do about Gaggenow?'

Harry's eyes narrowed.

'It's about time I had a word with the fish-faced kangaroo, that's what!' said Harry getting out of bed, a determined look on his face.

'Ewww – put some'

'clothes on first!' wailed the twins.

GAGGENOW was sitting in the galley, eating his lunch through a long straw, and making loud and disgusting sucking noises as he did so. Harry, now properly dressed, marched into the room, Barl by his side, Werdle and the twins hurrying along behind him.

'Gaggs, you scheming little fish-faced kangaroo! I want a word with you!'

Gaggenow looked up, his eyes widening in fear. Harry pointed an accusatory finger at him.

'Now listen here,' he began, but Gaggenow's eyes were fixed on Harry's hand. His squid finger was wobbling around weirdly... Harry shoved his hand into a pocket, used his other to gesticulate. But that hurt, so he just stood there instead. He'd already messed it up and he'd hardly begun!

'What is it, Harry?' said Gaggenow, looking at everyone's faces, as though trying to gauge the mood.

'I'll tell you what's the matter. You stole the Crown Starheart, and then stowed away on this ship, bringing all the bounty hunters in the universe – including the Leptira – down on our heads and—'

'Maybe – but if that hadn't happened the Greys would have thrown you into space, or put you to sleep or something, and you'd never have been captain!' interjected Gaggenow.

Harry glanced over at Werdle, the Grey. She was pretending to examine the back of her hand.

'Well, anyway. We only just managed to escape

– because of me, by the way—' continued Harry before he was interrupted again.

'And ended up marooned in the Void,' said Gaggenow. 'Because of you.'

'Yes, well – that reminds me! I got us out of there by doing that horrible deal with Ambassador Dee-ung, that weirdo Coagulite from Glob! And now I've got a little Coagulite worm actually inside of me, waiting to tell me when I've got to do what Dee-ung wants! Imagine how that would make you feel!' said Harry.[20]

'Price of leadership,' said Gaggenow with a shrug.

'Hah, easy for you to say. And then we get to the Leaf Star resort—'

'Which you nearly crashed into,' said Gaggs.

'Well, yeah, but we didn't actually crash, did we?' said Harry. 'And there, you tried to sell our ship from right under our noses, ripping the twins off,

---

20. The Coagulites are a race of blobby, brown shape changers who are famous as deal makers. They rescued Harry and his crew from the Void, but as part of a special deal. In return a semi-living worm-like creature was placed inside of Harry – it was actually a part of Dee-ung – ready to call in a favour when they needed it.

and attempting to leave me behind as well – as a servant!'

'Now, now, that was all a misunderstanding...' blustered Gaggenow, whilst at the same time trying to hide a mischievous grin.

'Hah! And then, after we get away – thanks to me again – you drug me whilst I'm asleep, strap me in an escape pod and maroon me on a miserable, wretched, mud-covered, superheavy-gravity planet full of huge-tongued monsters and three-legged murderous freaks wearing yellow stockings and—'

'Hey! That our home you talking about,' said Barl.

'Oh! Oh yes, sorry Barl, I didn't mean it like that, it's nice... Umm...' stammered Harry.

'See?' said Gaggenow. 'I did you a favour. That's where you met Barl, your son!'

Harry ignored him. 'And then you try to sell the twins! And you're such a scheming idiot you couldn't help yourself, and tried to sell them to the very same Leptiran nutters who've been chasing us all over space!'

'No, no, that was you!' said Gaggenow.

'Don't give me that, we know that's not true, we've

got proof!' said Harry. 'Show him, Dave!'

A holographic monitor appeared in the air and began to play back the video of Gaggenow trying to sell the twins.

Gaggenow's face turned a bright shade of yellow. 'Farglian fudge!' was all he could get out as he gulped.

'And then you get everyone captured, and I have to rescue you all – again, and—'

'Actually, I think you'll find that was really Werdle,' said Gaggenow, looking around wildly for an escape route.

Harry blinked. 'Well...yes, that's true, I suppose. But the point is that everything is your fault! Everything!'

Gaggenow looked up at him. And then away. And then to the ground.

'I'm sorry! I'm sorry,' he said at last, putting his hands over his head. 'It's just been so... I can't... I mean...'

And he began to cry – great heaving sobs. Harry put a hand up to his mouth. But then he realised he'd wrapped a bony, squid-like tentacle around his chin, and took it away. He sighed. That was the trouble with Gaggenow, he had this trick of making himself look so vulnerable, you couldn't help but feel sorry for him. At least, Harry was fairly certain it was a trick.

'It's been so awful, running and hiding and...you see, they've got my family,' sobbed Gaggenow.

'What do you mean? said Harry.

'My mum, my brother and my sisters, they've got them...and they threatened...' Gaggenow couldn't finish the sentence, he was so choked-up.

'Who's "they"?'

'Trust me, you don't want to know. They're as ruthless as a Leptiran at dinnertime,' said Gaggenow, 'and far more powerful.'

'So "they" said, "If you don't steal the Starheart for us, we'll kill your family," type of thing? Oh, Gaggs, I'm sorry,' said Harry, feeling rather guilty about it all now.

'What? NO, no! Not kill them... You see, my family, they're worse than I am. Much worse. No, they threatened to give them back...' said Gaggenow, looking up at Harry with tear-laden eyes.

'Wha...?' said a flabbergasted Harry.

'Umm...Captain?' said Dave the computer.

'Yes, Dave?'

'There's something... Oh my stars! WARNING, PROXIMITY ALERT, WARNING!'

'What's happening?' said Harry, confused.

'On the monitor, look!' said Dave.

Outside, next to the *Fartface Banana Nose*, something seemed to be materialising out of empty space. It was completely smooth, round and black. To Harry, it looked just like a great big black pool ball.

'Aieee!' said Gaggenow. 'It's a Stealth Hunter, de-cloaking!'

'A Stealth what?' said Harry.

'Hunter – a ship typically used by bounty hunters, pirates and smugglers. It can cloak itself and creep right up on you undetected!' said Dave. 'It's attached itself to the cargo bay hold, where the hull breach is. They can board us from there pretty easily.'

'To the cargo bay, everyone – we've got to stop them!' shouted Harry.

14 AN UNWANTED GUEST

HARRY, Barl, Werdle and the twins rushed into the cargo bay. Harry looked behind. No Gaggenow. Of course, what did he expect? It was probably just as well, mind, if it came to a fight.

At the far end of the bay was the hull breach, a big, ragged hole. Beyond it, a blue shimmering force field – what Dave called a Hermetic Force Bubble. Beyond that was the black, gleaming hull of the Stealth Hunter, connected to the *Fartface* by a pressurised docking collar. As they stepped forward the force field dissolved with a humming click.

They were too late. Something was entering the cargo hold – eight feet of walking titanium, by the look of it.

Tiny Tin, robot bounty hunter.

'Hand over Gaggenow and all his possessions, and I might let you live,' boomed the robot.

'Why can't you people just leave me alone?' said Harry, despairingly.

'That can be arranged. But you've got something that doesn't belong to you, and I want it!' said Tiny Tin, his voice grating mechanically.

'You can't just board people's ships and threaten them like this,' said Harry.

'It's just so'

'terribly rude,' said the twins.

'Just bring me the icthysupial and I'll be on my way,' said the robot. 'If not...well, I can't guarantee your safety.'

'Barl will smash,' said Barl, and he ran full tilt at the robot.

'Wait, don't!' said Harry but it was too late.

Tiny Tin turned to meet Barl's charge head-on but Barl smashed into the robot with such force that Tiny Tin fell sprawling to the ground in a clattering heap.

That wasn't what Harry had expected at all! He, Werdle and the twins all cheered as Barl straddled the robot, and raised his arms to smash down.

'Surrender, and Barl not smash you to dented

scrap!' he said, but Tiny Tin raised an arm, and something long, thin and needle-like shot out from a device on his metallic forearm, spearing Barl in his barrel torso, before retracting once more with a steely hum.

'NOOOOO!' screamed Harry, as Barl gasped in shock, and then slumped forward, unmoving. The twins raised their hands to their faces in horror, eyes wide and blinking from side to side rapidly, like lizards. Werdle gasped – and began to back away.

'What have you done?' screamed Harry, as he activated his sword. White hot rage filled his heart. He would kill that robot if it was the last thing he did.

Tiny Tin heaved Barl's body off himself, and got up with a clanking rattle. 'Don't worry,' said the robot. 'It's a special drug that will knock him out for a few hours – he'll be fine. I've got one for each of your species. Resistance will be ineffective.'

Harry felt both fear and relief at the same time – relief because Barl was alive and fear because Tiny Tin had a special knockout drug just for him too. Well, he'd see about that. He stepped forward, brandishing his sword. Tiny Tin looked down. Was that an expression on its robotic face? If so it was one of amused contempt.

'What are you going to do with that?' said the robot. 'Play a tune on my metal skin?'

'Yeah, some slash metal riffs, I reckon! It's a Survivor 2000 blade – Hub tech,' said Harry, taking another step forward.

'Hub tech, eh? Hmmm… OK, that would actually cut me up a bit, maybe take an arm off before I could inject you, but so what? I'm a robot, I'll just weld it back on later. And if, somehow, you're actually trained to use the sword – well, I don't have to use the drug, that's just me doing you a favour. I could blow you into space molecules with this,' said Tiny, showing another weapon strapped onto his other forearm, like a small gun. It had the words 'Deth Ray' written on it.

Harry blinked. 'That should say D-e-a-t-h Ray, surely?', he said.

'Whatever,' said the robot, aiming it at him.

Harry reviewed the situation. On his side were a single Grey and two Yureshtian twins.

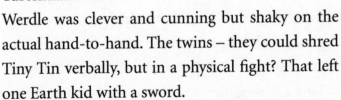

Werdle was clever and cunning but shaky on the actual hand-to-hand. The twins – they could shred Tiny Tin verbally, but in a physical fight? That left one Earth kid with a sword.

Versus an eight foot titanium robot who couldn't spell. Arg!

Suddenly a holographic monitor appeared in the air with Gaggenow's face on it.

'Hey, everyone, it's me!' said Gaggs. 'And look what I've got!'

He held up the Starheart. All eyes were on him.

'And look where I am!' Gaggenow gestured behind him – he was on the *Greene One*, Harry's other spaceship, the one he and Barl had been given from Tricrus. It was much smaller, much less advanced than the *Fartface Banana Nose*, but it had interstellar capability.

'Clever little hyperdrive type engine, this ship has, I must say. Just heading for the sun as I speak. I'm outta here. Goodbye, my little Farglian roaches!' said Gaggenow. And the monitor went dead.

Tiny Tin froze for a second. His head began to whirr loudly, and suddenly he turned and rushed back to the airlock and into his ship without a word.

'Dave, reseal the cargo hold now!' said Harry.

The blue force bubble went back up just in time, as Tiny Tin shot off into space in his Stealth Hunter in pursuit of Gaggenow.

Harry heaved a sigh of relief, as he and Werdle went over to check on Barl. He seemed fine. In fact, he was snoring.

Werdle looked up at Harry. 'Do you think Gaggenow has finally done the right thing?'

'What do you mean?' said Harry.

'Well...he could have just left in the *Greene One*. He didn't have to tell us he was going. More importantly, he let Tiny Tin know, so that he'd chase after him,' said Werdle thoughtfully.

'Do you know, Werdle, I think you're right! He actually saved us, and got himself into trouble in the process,' said Harry.

'There's a first time for everything, I suppose,' said Werdle.

'Still, knowing Gaggenow'

'it's probably not quite'

'so simple,' said the twins.

'True...but then again...what's the trick? No, I think he finally felt bad about what he'd done to me – us – and...incredibly, did the right thing,' said Harry.

'Hmmm...'

'We'll see,' said the twins.

'Indeed we shall,' said Dave the computer over the intercom. 'Well, Captain, both the *Greene One* and the Stealth Hunter are out of sensor range. The Leptiran battle cruiser is still disabled. We are on our own and safe for now. Gaggenow and the Starheart are no longer with us.'

'Which means we're no long public enemy number one!' said Harry.

'Well, we're still probably in the top ten,' said Werdle, 'but at least they won't be chasing us so hard for a while!'

'Where to, Captain?' said Dave.

'Now that Gaggenow's gone with the Starheart, we can go... Well, I'd like to go to Volans,' said Harry.

'Volans?' said the twins together.

'Yeah. You know where that is, don't you Werdle?' said Harry

'Where the Wagglestaff Corporation is based? Sure, I know where that is – most of the galaxy does,' says Werdle.

'You can lead us there?' said Harry.

'I can put that in the navigation computers, no problem. But why Volans?' said Werdle.

'Wagglestaff own the *Supernova*, and Colum the Columnite reporter works for the *Supernova*, and I'm pretty sure she knows where Earth is!' said Harry excitedly.

'So that's what this is all about,'

'you just want to go home,' said the twins.

'Yeah,' said Harry.

'What about us?' said Alph at the same time as Bet said, 'But what about me?'

'Well,' said Harry, '...err...what would you like to do?'

The twins looked at each other and shrugged.

'You could come to Earth with me,' said Harry.

'Earth? Oh, come on,'

'it's a primitive backwater,'

'what would we do there'

'once we've got bored with'

'the quaint little monkey people and'

'their primitive art?' said the twins.

Harry folded his arms and sighed. 'OK, well, lets go to Volans and decide there. I could drop you off at Yureshto on the way to Earth or something.'

'What, just like that?' said the twins together.

'Well...yes, if you want, I guess,' said Harry.

'Fine,'

'forget it, then,' said the twins, and they stomped off, marching in unison, hand in hand.

Harry stared after them, frowning in puzzlement.

Werdle was looking at him from the corner of her eye, a half smile on her turnip shaped head.

'What?' said Harry.

'Nothing, nothing!' she said.

'Well...what about you, Werdle, what do you want?' said Harry.

'Not sure. Maybe to get back to Canus Prime, my homeworld. I'll probably have to get a job first. Volans is good, though, there's a big Grey embassy there, so you can drop me off. I'll be fine.'

'OK, that's cool,' said Harry. 'Though I'll miss you!'

'Thanks. But will you miss the twins?' said Werdle.

'I guess...if truth be told...I think I will,' said Harry.

'Maybe you should tell them that,' said Werdle.

'Crumbs, no!' said Harry. 'I wouldn't hear the end of it if I told them! They'd rip me to shreds.'

'Well, anyway. Before we go anywhere I'm going to visit the AutoDoc, if that's OK with you, Captain. It's time I got a new arm!' said Werdle.

'Oh yes, of course! Sorry, Werdle, we'll wait for you before we do anything.' Harry had completely forgotten that poor old Werdle had lost an arm to the Leptira. He'd been hogging the AutoDoc, and with everything happening so fast there'd been no time for Werdle to get any treatment. It was her turn.

'Though...do you think it's safe?' said Harry.

'Seems to be pretty good at regenerating Grey limbs and appendages, so yes!' said Werdle jauntily.

'**SO,**' said Harry, as he walked onto the bridge, 'how did it go?'

Werdle sat in the navigation chair, one arm inputting information into the navigation computers, the other hidden behind a grey cape with silver edgings that was thrown over one shoulder. 'What? How did what go?' said Werdle grumpily.

'You know, the AutoDoc. Your arm?' said Harry.

Werdle glared at him. 'Bah!' was all she said.

'What?' said Harry.

Werdle made a sign with her hand, a kind of wobbly writhing of her squid fingers, held up in the air and waved from side to side.

'Eh?' said Harry.

Dave spoke into his ear. 'That's the five-fingered writhe, as the Greys call it. Basically sticking your fingers up at someone, like you do on Earth.'

'Hey, what did I do?' said Harry.

'Infected the AutoDoc with your DNA is what you did,' said Werdle, throwing off her cape and revealing a new arm. It was smaller than the other and a bit stunted, but worst of all...

It was human.

'Hah, hah, hah!' Harry laughed at the sight of it, without thinking.

'Oh, glad you think it's funny,' said Werdle, pulling up her cape over her mutant arm.

Harry blinked. 'Sorry. But you laughed at my hand!'

'Yeah, your little finger. This is a whole arm. And it's not even the right size!'

'Can you get it fixed?' said Harry.

Werdle sighed. 'Dave advises that it's best just to keep away from the AutoDoc for now. Until proper repairs can be done. So no.'

'Well, that leaves us lumbered with what

we've got, then,' said Harry.

'Yup. Until we get to Volans,' said Werdle looking up.

'Really?' said Harry.

'The Grey embassy there, it's a full-on enclave. They've got all the up to date, state-of-the-art stuff – they'll be able to fix me up... They might even be able to fix you, maybe,' said Werdle.

'Well then, the quicker we get there the better! So, to Volans, and don't spare the horses, Dave!' said Harry.

'Errr...we don't have any native-to-Earth quadruped, ungulate mammals on board, Harry,' said Dave.

'No, no...never mind, Dave, just get us there as fast as you can,' said Harry.

'Are you sure? That could damage the engines, and I don't see any imminent threats – is that an order, Captain?' said Dave.

'Right, get us there as quickly as possible without doing any damage to the ship in any way, OK?' said Harry, calling up his GalNav tracker as he did so. It was time to check out Volans.

Volans

Named for its discoverer, Arminius Armpitbreath Volans III, the planet was an uninhabited wasteland, a dead planet and pretty worthless when first found, until they discovered Jargonium[21] — vast reserves of it. Then it was colonised, but mostly as a mining installation. Later, its location became important as a border post between two ancient empires. Eventually, it became a vital trading planet. So it got terra-formed, and millions came to live there.

Then those two empires quarrelled. There was a huge war that left Volans devastated and pitted with vast canyons and great craters. But that was long ago.

The planet has been relandscaped since then and the craters and canyons are now celebrated as wonders. So Volans has become one of the biggest trading and tourist centres in the Hub.

---

21. A rare metal used in Hyper Drive Engines

Species

There are no species native to Volans. All life was brought here from the rest of the galaxy. But now it teems with billions of creatures of all kinds from all over the universe. A kind of 'native' (i.e. those born on Volans) culture has grown up, though, marked by its extreme use of language, especially adjectives.

HARRY, Werdle, Barl, Alph and Bet stepped out of the airlock door and into the entrance corridor that led to the Volans spaceport. Harry had paid his docking fee, and bought some energy cells for the Fusion Banks. He'd lodged his ship's owner certificate with the relevant authorities and ticked all the right bureaucratic boxes. That had cost 2,500 credits, leaving him with 500. Not much, but he still had a cargo of Grerk. He just hoped that was worth something.

They entered the 'Inordinate and Extravagant Security Verification Meticulous Search and Certify Most Thoroughly Zone'.

Crazy name, Harry thought.

Inside were huge battle robots with ultra-sensitive sensors that could detect anything from explosives to the wrong kind of fruit, or even the wrong kind of fly or ant. Fortunately Harry and his party were all clean.

183

They continued on and emerged into the spaceport itself...

Harry had been amazed at the Haddus Prime spaceport but this was something else. Volans was a major planet in the Hub, both as a commercial and

a tourist destination and its spaceport reflected that. Its full name was the Astonishing Volans Interstellar Spaceport of Incredible Amazement and it was much as its title suggested – huge, sprawling and quite astonishing. Everywhere teemed a vast array of aliens of all sorts and sizes.

Barl and Harry stared around, slack-jawed at the sight of it. Werdle, who'd seen it all before, of course, carefully adjusted her cape to cover her human arm. The twins' eyes were wide with excitement. What a sight!

All around milled crowds, travelling about on an array of mechanical walkways and escalators. Some 'walkways' were actually rushing streams, with different liquids for the various aquatic aliens. Others were floating walkways or moving pavements. There were also mechanical hover boards that would take you where you asked them to, as well as 'balloon taxis', car-sized zeppelins that you could hitch rides on, floating up and around and all over the vast space. Shops and restaurants were everywhere.

The noise was overwhelming. Hundreds of

different alien species all talking, clicking, warbling, trumpeting, ringing, tweeting or blowing, in a cacophony of sound.

'Wow...' muttered Harry.

'Incredible place'

'for shopping'

'if we had'

'any money,' said the twins. And they looked over at Harry reproachfully.

'Hey, earn your own money!' said Harry.

'We are royalty,'

'we never work,' said the twins haughtily.

'Oh please, you're cloned fake royals, you mean!' said Harry.

'How dare you?'

'If you were'

'a true gentleman,'

'you'd fund us in the style'

'we deserve!' they said.

'Oh-ho, I should just give you money, should I?'

'See,' said Alph to Bet, 'he's too low class'

'to even understand the concept,' continued Bet.

'Oh, for goodness sake! Here, take this,' said

Harry, and he gave them 50 credits each.

The twins looked down at the money in their hands, looked up at Harry, looked back at the credits...

And dropped the money on the floor with expressionless faces, turning away as if Harry did not exist.

'Why you little...' muttered Harry, picking it up off the floor.

'How could you insult'

'us with such derisory sums?' said the twins, walking on.

Harry sighed. Werdle looked on with a wry grin. Barl scratched his head.

As they set off after the twins an alien frog creature glided past, just like the one that had given Harry the message from Werdle at Haddus Prime spaceport.

'*Supernova*, *Supernova*, get your *Supernova* here!' croaked the frog messenger.

'Arg, I can't stand frogs! Barl, can you get one of those for us?' said Harry.

'Sure thing, Ma,' said Barl, 'it a good read!'

THE SUPERNOVA[22]

Gossip Column   07.14.4056 GMT

With Editor-in-Chief Ratchet Pliers, a Wordsmith 6000 Artificial Editorial Solution Bot. Hacking you all the Supernova *gossip from databanks all over the galaxy![23]*

01011100101100[24], everyone!

Guess what, biologically configured freaks... Colum the Columnite Columnist from Caryatid has been arrested. Yes, it's true. Hub authorities will not tell us why, either. Is this an attack on press freedom? Hard to say... I mean, actually hard to say, as to make that claim is illegal. So I won't say it.

Bail has been set at 100,000 Galactic Credits – a huge amount, so if there are any millionaires out there who would like to pay on our behalf, the staff at the Supernova *would be grateful.*

Make payment to: The Money Counting Acceptors of Court Bail and Fine Payments Kind of Thing at Volans Supreme Legal Adjudicating Courthouse of Legal Stuff in Big Fat City.

---

22. The *Supernova* is a fully owned subsidiary of the Wagglestaff Corporation
23. In accordance with all Imperial and Hub nexus laws of course. Completely.
24. Cybernetic greetings, bio-units!

Now, on to other things.

Coaguwhats?

The Awesomely Equanimous Plenipotentiary Dee-Ung, of the Globular Consulate has come to the Hub! He's the Ambassador of Cool from Glob, and he's a Coagulite. You remember them? Balls of mud that can pretty much shape themselves into anything they like. Usually they stay out of Hub politics, but seems like they're taking more of an interest in our affairs these days. They want to set up more trade and cultural links and all that. But watch out if you want to make a deal with them. They're sticklers for it — most of their contracts are in small print, with sub-clauses on their sub-clauses!
And then there's the 'Indentursite' — a little brown worm, like an enforceable contract wriggling around inside you. What kind of bacteria-brained idiot would accept that as a deal, eh?

001010110101[25], until next time, biologically configured freaks!

---

25. 'Goodbye', but literally translated as 'switching users until reboot'.

'Well, if that doesn't take the Farglian roach biscuit,' said Harry. 'Typical!'

'What's the matter?' said Werdle.

'The person...err...being...I want to talk to has been arrested. Just my luck! The bail's 100,000 credits and right now, well, I've got 500,' said Harry with a shake of the head.

'And a cargo of Grerk. That's worth quite a bit, you know. You should go and sell it,' said Werdle.

'Good idea – there's got to be somewhere here to do that, right?'

'Yes, the assay office. Or, as they call it, the "Established Company Offices of Buying and Selling Interstellar Goods with Legalised Transactions, Style of Thing". Over there,' she said, pointing off to the right.

'I'll just call it the assay office, I think. Anyway, let's go,' said Harry.

'Not me, Harry, I'm off to the Grey enclave. Got to get my arm sorted. And then – well, I need a job or something. Or maybe I'll go home to Canus if I can get a lift.'

'Oh, right, of course,' said Harry. 'Umm...thanks

for everything, Werdle, you've been...'

'Yes, well. I'll be at the enclave for a while yet, – come and visit me if you like. Maybe I can sort that finger for you as well,' said Werdle.

'But...won't the other Greys want their ship back?' said Harry.

'What? Oh no! Don't worry about that – they sell those ships all over the place, and you've got a genuine certificate of ownership. They won't think anything of it. Well, unless I told them, of course, but don't worry, I won't do that, I promise!'

'OK, thanks again, then, and good luck,' said Harry.

'Well, if I don't see you, hope you make it back to your mum, and sorry about... Well, you know. Bye, Barl. Bye, Alph and Bet!' said Werdle.

'See you,' said Barl.

'Goodbye and'

'good luck!' said the twins.

Harry watched Werdle go, her cape slung over one shoulder like a tiny musketeer. She was the last of her original crew. She'd been kidnapped by the Leptira, tortured, and then had her arm eaten.

She'd lost her spaceship to a human boy from Earth, and now had a copy of his arm as her own. Yet she seemed pretty cool about it all. OK, part of that was probably guilt for having abducted him from home in the first place, but still...

He was going to miss her.

17 BEYOND THE DREAMS OF AVARICE

HARRY sat at his console in the Captain's Cabin. He opened up Galnet, and navigated to the Grand Bank of Volans personal accounts login page.

He started to login with his account details. Name – Captain Harry Greene. Passcode: 0407AG85. His birthday, 4th July. American Independence Day, which made it easy to remember. The rest was simply the old name of the *Fartface* before he'd changed it.

And the final login detail? The password: Ariadne. His mum's first name. Up came his details.

Account holder: Captain Harry Greene
Account Type: Much Revered Super Beloved Customer Premium Account
Account Number: 0783392666/HG
Balance: 1,000,000 Galactic Credits

Harry stared at it in delight, and sniggered. A million credits! He could hardly believe it, but there it was, on the screen.

He was a Galactic millionaire!

Technically, he would be called a 'Grerk millionaire'. It turned out Big Fat City on Volans was going through a Grerk craze right now, and Harry had turned up with a cargo load of it at just the right time. He'd sold the lot for a million. Of course, he hadn't mentioned that Grerk was the dung of the Haddusian monkey-mole.

Grerk millionaire? Poo millionaire, more like!

Harry laughed out loud at the thought. Maybe finally his luck was changing. If he could get home now – well, his mum wouldn't have to live in a council flat any more. He could buy her... Harry frowned. He didn't think there was an actual exchange rate for pounds and Galactic Credits, though. But still.

Anyway, first things first. He had things to do. He had to pay Colum the Columnite's bail. He'd gone to the court and arranged for her release after selling his cargo, but couldn't make payment until the money was in his account. Now it was, so he transferred 100,000 credits to the Volans Court account. Colum would be freed as soon as it cleared, hopefully in a couple of hours. She'd agreed to come to the ship and meet Harry, her unexpected benefactor, as soon as they let her out of jail.

Next job – 'Operation Blue Happiness', as Harry called it. He hit the button on the 3D Grand Bank Credit Chip Printer he'd installed on his console. He watched his account tick down a little as it printed out several rectangular plastic credit chips, threaded with some kind of metallic stuff from the bank's printer. Credit chips, several thousand Galactic Credits worth of them. Out here, instead of going to a cashpoint, you just printed out your own money – how cool was that? Well, you could if you had a Much Revered blah blah account, of course. And he did! Harry sniggered to himself again. He couldn't help it. He was rich!

He swept up the chips and hurried out the door, heading for the twins' cabin. He knocked on their door.

'Yes, who is it?'

'We're watching a Holovid!' said the twins.

'It's me, Harry,' he said.

'Yes...?'

'We're busy!' came the answer.

'Come on, open the door, I've got a present for you!' said Harry.

'Really? Well, in'

'that case, do come in!' said the twins, and the door opened with a swish.

Harry walked into their cabin. The walls were the regulation gleaming grey steel with black trim, but the twins had hung up artfully placed drapes and rugs on the walls and floor. Various pictures were hung in perfect artistic harmony, mostly in white, blue and gold.

Harry glanced at the Holovid. They were watching something called *Attack of the Colonial Space Marines*. It appeared to be some kind of horror film, about a poor tribe of egg-laying creatures who lived on a planet inside lots of tunnels, and a cruel group of alien humanoid marines, decked out in battle tech from head to foot, who turn up and begin slaughtering the creatures in droves.

'I didn't know you were into science fiction films!' said Harry surprised.

'What is'

'science fiction?' said the twins.

'Umm...forget it. Let me start again, umm… I didn't know you were into horror films!'

'Oh yes, we like'

'them a lot.'

'Anyway, what was that'

'about a present?' said the twins.

'Oh yeah! Here you go,' said Harry, and he handed them each 10,000 credits worth of Credit chips.

The twins looked at the chips, their golden eyes widening into hugeness. They almost seemed to give off beams of golden light. They looked up at Harry, looked back at the chips, then up at Harry again.

'Is this'

'a joke?' they said hesitantly, as if they couldn't quite bring themselves to believe it.

'Nope. There it is. 10K each – go shopping! Go on, both of you, on me!' said Harry, grinning like an idiot.

The twins' jaws dropped. 'It's really real?' they said together.

'YES! Go on, shop 'til you drop!' said Harry.

Both of them shrieked in delight, and sped past him on either side, heading for the door. Suddenly they pulled up short, turned, and each gave Harry a kiss on the cheek at once, almost squashing his head between them. Then they rushed off with a shouted, 'Not bad – for an Earth boy!' followed by peals of laughter.

Not exactly the thanks he'd been hoping for, but still. Harry smiled.

It didn't matter. Things were going so well. Harry turned and set off after them. It was time to go and see Werdle.

Harry took a floating blimp taxi to the Grey embassy enclave in Big Fat City. Big Fat City itself was indeed big. All the buildings were huge, and also, well, fat. Most buildings were kind of pear-shaped, with round balls on top, as if the city was made up of thousands of big fat babies, just sitting there. The Grey Embassy, though, was different. It was a wide, one-storied wheel-shaped building of grey steel, with a long staircase leading up to the front door. Built by Greys for Greys.

Harry walked through the big grey steel doors and up to the embassy counter.

'Yep?' said a Grey peremptorily, without even looking up.

'Captain Greene, come to see a friend of mine,' said Harry.

'Try the canteen – everyone's at lunch,' said the Grey, still without even looking at him. Harry looked around. A big sign said:

THE GREY CAFE
GREY SLUDGE AT GREY PRICES

It didn't sound very appetising. Anyway, he walked in. It was full of Greys having lunch – at least a hundred of them! Harry looked around. They all looked pretty much the same to him. But only one of them would have a human arm, or a cape covering it. But he couldn't see Werdle. Unless she'd already had her arm fixed?

'Excuse me, everyone, sorry to bother you!' shouted Harry at the top of his voice. All the Greys turned to look at him, their big eyes black and unblinking. It was a bit creepy, actually, like being in a room with a hundred cats all staring at you silently.

'I'm looking for Werdle? Anyone here called Werdle?' shouted Harry at the top of his voice.

About fifty Greys put their hands up.

'Yeah, me.'

'I'm Werdle.'

'That's my name,' came a chorus of voices.

'Which number, you idiot?' said a nearby Grey. 'There are hundreds of Werdles, for Grey's sake.'

Harry blinked, stupefied for a moment. 'Oh yeah...umm...WERDLE...errr...412, that's it. 412!' shouted Harry.

A Grey at the back of the room leaned back in her chair and hollered at someone. '412, it's for you!' And out from behind the crowd came Werdle.

'Werdle, it's me, Harry!' said Harry.

She waved him over and soon they were seated on their own table in a corner of the canteen.

'So,' said Harry, 'looks like you got your arm fixed?'

'Yes,' said Werdle, holding up her new Grey arm. 'Works perfectly, thanks.'

'Can they fix my finger, then?' said Harry.

Werdle scrunched up her turnip head in a Grey expression of uncertainty. 'Well, probably, but it would cost quite a bit, and take about a month. They'd have to sequence your DNA and—'

'A month? Don't think I can wait that long,' said Harry. 'Maybe if someone could fix up the AutoDoc on the *Fartface* I could get it done there. I also need someone to fix the hull.'

'Well, you'd need a trained engineer for that, and you need some Canusium for the hull,' said Werdle.

'Surely I can buy Canusium here? And maybe hire an engineer – you're looking for work, right?'

'Yes, you can, but that costs, and you haven't... Wait, did you sell the Grerk?' said Werdle.

'Yup!' said Harry. 'For a load of credits! Want to work for me, Werdle? I can pay you a proper wage and everything!'

'What...4,000 credits a month?' said Werdle.

'Done!' said Harry.

'Arg, I should have asked for more!' said Werdle.

18 DRESSING UP DOLL

HARRY was in his cabin. Werdle, his chief engineer (he had a chief engineer!) was in the damaged cargo hold, supervising the delivery of Canusium metal he'd bought, before beginning the task of fixing it up. Then she'd take a look at the AutoDoc.

For now, Harry was waiting for Colum the Columnite Columnist from Caryatid who should be turning up soon. There was a knock on the door.

'Yeah, come in,' said Harry, and the door swished aside at his command.

But it wasn't Colum, it was the twins. They were smiling happily, eyes shining like gold, blue skin glowing like sapphires, their hair done up stylishly. They were wearing new clothes, Volans style – voluminous white robes over billowing white trousers, with golden accessories.

'Hello, Harry,' said the twins. 'What do you think?' they said together and twirled. Their robes billowed out and around them like fluffy white heavenly clouds lined with blue and gold.

They looked fantastic, Harry had to admit.

He couldn't help himself and said, 'You look... amazing.' He wasn't sure he should be telling them that. Maybe he should be playing it cool.

'At last, common as muck'

'Earth boy recognises his superiors,' said the twins, but at least this time they said it with smiles.

Harry raised his eyes. He'd just given them 20,000 credits, and it seemed like all that had changed was that he got smiles instead of mocking sneers when they were teasing him. *Well, thank heaven for small mercies, I suppose,* he thought.

'But we don't think'

'you should be a'

'common Earth boy any more'

'if you're going to be our friend!' said the twins.

'Friend?' said Harry. This was an unexpected turn!

'Yes, quite so.'

'You can't go around'

'dressed in those primitive'

'monkey clothes any more!' they said.

Bet took out a special-looking box labelled The Voice of Volans Vogue.

'If you are to be our captain'

'then you have to look the part.'

'So we got you this'

'from the most fashionable shop'

'on the planet!' said the twins, bringing out a set of clothes.

It was a captain's suit – some kind of space-navy captain's suit... Harry couldn't believe it. It looked something like this:

'I can't wear that!' he said.

'Oh, yes you can,' said the twins advancing on him with sartorial intent.

And they dressed him as if he was a doll, giggling the whole time. Harry wanted to resist, but...well, the outfit was kind of cool and the twins seemed to be having fun. And they were being nice to him.

'There you are!'

'Have a look'

'in the mirror,' they said.

Harry checked it out. He couldn't help himself and strutted a bit. It was a great outfit, like some kind of steampunk imperial-space-navy thing. But then he had a thought. He wasn't role-playing, was he? He actually was a starship captain. He could wear this because it was real. He didn't have to pretend.

'Here, put on the cap,' said the twins.

Harry put it on his head – but it was too big and fell down over his eyes. The twins burst out laughing. Was that it, then, thought Harry, all this just for the cap joke?

But Bet took the cap off, made some adjustments,

and put it back on his
head at a jaunty angle.

They stepped back.

'Oh my, you look
quite'

'the dashing
captain,' said the twins.

'Really?' said Harry.

'Yes, really –'

'for a primitive
Earth boy!' said the
twins, laughing, but
they said it with far

less venom than usual, and the laughter didn't have
the usual mocking tones. It was almost affectionate.

Almost.

Harry looked in the mirror. He couldn't help
himself and preened some more. He looked so
cool! Like an officer from *Star Wars* or... Hold on!
Quickly he glanced over at the twins. This had to be
some kind of trick, right?

But no...they were gazing at him as if he really
did look good.

'Now you are'

'worthy to be seen'

'with us,' said the twins.

'Oh, I see,' said Harry, 'that's what this is about.'

'Of course! As royalty'

'it's perfectly respectable'

'to be seen with a'

'starship captain,' said the twins.

Harry shook his head. They were such snobs! But still, he had to admit, he liked it. And if it meant they'd stop taking the mickey out of him so much, all the better.

Harry smiled a wry smile. 'Why, thank you,' he said.

Dave's voice sounded over the intercom. 'There's someone here to see you, Captain, someone called Colum. She's in the cargo bay, waiting for you. Just walked in, it seems.'

'Walked in?'

'Well, there's a big hole in the hull, isn't there? And the force field's been turned off for Werdle to work on it. People are walking by and gawping. Sooner it's fixed the better!'

'OK, Dave, I'm on my way,' said Harry.

'Hold on, we haven't'

'finished dressing you up, yet.'

'We've got all your'

'casual wear clothes'

'to put on,' said the twins, holding up more outfits.

'Thanks a lot, honestly, I love the clothes, but I have to go,' said Harry.

'Awww...' said the twins. 'What a pity. You really are a most excellent dressing up doll.'

I guess it's a kind of promotion, from primitive Earth boy to dressing up doll with a rank, thought Harry as he walked on down to the cargo bay, a half smile on his face. And the outfit felt pretty good. He definitely felt taller, like a real captain. It was amazing how a set of clothes could make you feel different about things. And the twins seemed sincere enough, even if it was just so that they didn't feel quite so embarrassed by him.

Harry smoothed out his jacket and he walked tall into the cargo bay. Overhead, up in the ceiling, a long gantry walkway had some heavy crates hanging from it and was slowly moving forward to the far end. The crates were labelled 'Canusium', the same metal as the ship was made from, and Werdle needed it to make repairs.

'Snappy suit, Captain,' said Dave the computer,

in his ear. 'Thank the stars it's self cleaning – you'll need that feature.'

'Yeah, thanks, Dave,' said Harry.

At the far end of the cargo bay, near the ruptured hull were Barl and Werdle – Chief Engineer Werdle, rather. They'd been unpacking one of the crates. And next to them was a pile of rubble.

Odd, thought Harry. He'd thought Canusium was a kind of metal – surely it should come in bars or something?

As he drew near, the rubble moved, swivelling round to face him.

'Ah, you must be Captain Greene,' grated a voice like a blender full of pebbles. 'I am Colum, pleased to meet you...' And the pile of rubble extended an arm in greeting.

She did indeed look like a heaped up pile of stones and rocks, with a round section of stone, a bit like a chunk of ancient Greek pillar, on top, for a head – with eyes in it. Big, girly eyes with make-up. And a stony mouth with stony lips. Painted red.

Harry shook his head in amazement.

'Errr...' rumbled Colum. 'Maybe I should...as

211

you're a...you know.' And she saluted him!

Cool, thought Harry – this captain's outfit really worked.

Werdle put her hands on her hips. 'Nice suit, Captain,' she said wryly, with an amused gleam in her eye.

Mind you, she'd still called him Captain, thought Harry.

'Yeah, nice outfit, Mum!' said Barl.

Colum turned to look at Barl. She raised a single, rocky eyebrow.

'Mum? My pebbles, wha...?' she mumbled.

212

'It's complicated,' said Harry. 'Anyway, welcome aboard the *Far*...errr...welcome aboard our ship, Colum!'

'Nice to meet you, Captain Greene, and so kind of you to bail me out. Please don't be offended if I cut the small talk, and get straight to the point – *why* did you bail me out?'

'We're all great fans of the *Supernova* – we love your column,' Harry began. 'In fact, I've got quite a few issues in my collection.'

'Me too!' said Barl.

'That's all very well, but 100K worth of fandom? Really?' said Colum.

'Errr no...' Harry coughed. 'Actually I wanted to know... Well, you know that piece you wrote about toast? It sweeping the galaxy and that?'

'Yeah...' said Colum.

'It's from Earth, isn't it?'

'Toast? Yes, it's from a planet called Earth,' said Colum. 'How'd you know?'

'That's where I'm from,' said Harry, 'and I'd like to go home but I don't know where it is.'

'You don't know where your home planet is?' said

Colum, looking him up and down.

Harry put a hand to his chin. Colum once again raised a rocky eyebrow and her pebble eyes widened.

'What...?' said Harry. 'Oh!' Quickly he put his hand behind his back. Blasted squid finger!

'I...it's a long story, but basically, no, I don't know where it is, and I was hoping you could tell me.'

Colum stared at him for a moment. 'Must be one hell of a story,' she said.

'Yeah, it sure is!' said Barl and Werdle together. They looked at each other and laughed.

'Well, maybe you'll tell me about it one day,' said Colum, 'me being a journalist and everything.'

'Maybe,' said Harry. 'So, then. Do you?'

'Do I what?'

'Know where Earth is,' said Harry.

'Oh yes, I do actually – ah, so that's why you bailed me out!' said Colum.

Harry's heart began to beat faster. At last, could it be that he was going to find his way home?

'Yes, I figured you might know. So...where is it?' said Harry.

'There's this guy...well, Space Scout they call

214

them. Explorers...they look for new planets. This one was called Arminius Armpitbreath Volans the 45th. This planet's named after his great, great, great etc grandfather from way back when. The family have been explorers for generations.'

'Yes, yes, go on,' said Harry.

'He discovered your planet a while back. Said it was...well, kinda primitive, with barely intelligent humanoid life... Umm... I mean, that's what he said, you know...'

'Yes, yes, I get it. I get it all the time, actually, so, where is it?' said Harry.

'He'd wandered about amongst the inhabitants, for a while. Hideous creatures apparently, all soft and blubbery like hairy-topped slugs on legs. Come to think of it, a bit like you, in fact. Anyway, he said the only thing he liked was toast, something he was given in...what was it...the Wind Sore Cough? No, Kaff? In a place called Slowe. Or Sluff, or something. Wind Sore Cough. Slau?'

'Ahhh.... Probably the Windsor Cafe, Slough,' said Harry.

'Whatever. Anyway, here, give me your GalNav

Tracker, I'll input the coordinates,' rattled Colum. 'It's the least I can do.'

Harry handed it over. Colum pounded some numbers in and then handed it back. Harry took it with trembling hands. Finally, he'd found it! After all this time, all this adventure, after so many brushes with death, someone had casually typed it into his Tracker, just like that. Now he could go home. Harry checked the GalNav. Yes, there it was, orbiting a yellow sun, third planet out of nine, blue and green, like a vision of heaven!

Hmm...actually, it might take a while to get back there. Earth was on the other side of the galaxy, it seemed, on the Far Side, as they called it. But then again, the *Fartface's* quantum drive was easily up to the job. It'd just take several jumps, and maybe a stop off for fuel along the way.

'Thank you,' said Harry, his voice choked. 'Thank you so much!'

'Hey, thank *you*! I'd have told you where Earth is for 50 credits, let alone 100,000!' said Colum.

'Well now, isn't this nice,' said a voice.

20 A MATTER OF SERIOUS GRAVITY

EVERYONE turned as three figures strolled into the cargo bay through the hole in the hull.

'That hole is really getting on my nerves,' muttered Dave the computer into Harry's earpiece.

Harry turned to the intruders and shouted, 'Hey, you can't just walk in here like that – this is my ship!'

'Oh, I think I can,' said the central figure, in a silky, confident voice.

Harry stared in astonishment. It was an Oryctonite – a race famous throughout the galaxy as the bureaucrats and civil servants of the Imperium. The race that ran the Hub...

Except that they looked to Harry like great big talking rabbits. White rabbits, just like from *Alice in Wonderland*, with big buck teeth (three instead of two, mind you) and floppy rabbity ears. But this one wasn't wearing a waistcoat with a watch. Instead

it had a long, purple-trimmed, bright white coat, like an admiral's, covered with badges and medals, and black-and-purple baggy leggings ending in chunky metallic boots. It wore some kind of hi-tech headgear, complete with a big, gold symbol on it – the symbol of the Hub Imperium.

On either side of him stood two figures, in armoured battle suits. Hub-tech armoured battle suits. They looked quite small but their heads were visored and bristling with tech and their power armour thrummed with energy. Each held big energy weapons, like laser rifles or something. They looked really, really bad-ass.

'Plodington Plods!' hissed Colum in astonishment.

Harry thought for a moment she was swearing, but actually, it was a name that rang a bell.

'With some Guardian Commandos!' warbled Werdle.

'Yes, indeed, Colum, it is I, Plodington Plods, Vizier Vexillarius, and second-in-command to the Galactic Overlord himself – who's an idiot, by the way, so it's me that gets everything done...' said the Vizier, and he gestured.

The two Guardians raised their rifles.

Harry's jaw dropped in astonishment. He *had* heard that silly name before. Plodington Plods. The Vizier. Number two in the whole hierarchy of the Empire. What was the second most powerful being in the galaxy doing on his ship?'

Colum gulped stonily. Barl and Werdle froze in shock.

'So, you must be Harry Greene... I'm sorry, Captain Harry Greene,' said the rabbity Vizier.

'Errr...yes, yes I am. What can I do for you... umm...sir?'

'First, you will call me your Excellency. Second, you will give me the Crown Starheart. Now. Or my Guardians will obliterate you. All of you.'

'I haven't got it!' said Harry.

'That's: "I haven't got it, your Excellency,"' said the Vizier.

'Why are you here, your Excellency? I mean, why you personally?' said Colum.

The Vizier glared at Colum. 'Bah, you should still be in jail!'

'So it was you who had me arrested! And I thought with what I know about the Starheart, you'd have been on my side,' said Colum.

'You know too much!' said the Vizier, giving her a hard stare.

'Well, I suppose I do know what it really does, and I know—' But before Colum could finish the sentence, the Vizier gestured at one of his Guardians, who raised his rifle and fired.

'Oh my pebbles!' was all that Colum got out before a bolt of yellow energy blasted her into bits, scattering shards of stone around the floor.

'Now she's toast,' said the Vizier.

'Crumbs!' said Harry, stepping back in horror.

Werdle turned to flee. Barl growled.

'Nobody move!' said Plodington Plods, and the Guardians trained their weapons on Harry, Werdle and Barl.

'You...murdered her!' said Harry.

'Oh, please, don't be ridiculous,' said Plodington. 'She's a Caryatid. They're not so easy to kill – her pebbles and rocks and so forth will gather themselves back together in no time and she'll be fine. Then... well, we'll see. You have to grind them into dust to really kill them.'

As the Vizier talked, Harry noticed some movement up above and behind him. He glanced up. There! The twins, on the gantry walkway. Slowly walking along, still dressed in their billowing white robes, looking like fluffy clouds drifting across the sky. What were they up to?

'Right, well, that's her out of the way. Now, once again, Captain. Bring me the Starheart, or I'll kill you all.'

'But your Excellency, I really haven't got it!' said Harry.

'Don't make me waste my time having to search the ship after my Guardians have smeared you all over the floor with their plasma rifles! Now, for the last time, where is the Crown Starheart, you wretched little worm?' said Plodington Plods.

'Gaggenow took it!' said Harry desperately.

'Right, kill them, kill them all,' said the Vizier.

'Wait!' said Harry, putting up a hand. 'Just wait! I can prove it to you, your Excellency.'.

'Stop!' said the Vizier to his soldiers. And then to Harry, 'Go on, then, prove it.'

Up above, Harry could see that the twins had manoeuvred a couple of crates of Canusium steel so they were right over the heads of the Guardians. *Brilliant,* thought Harry.

'Dave, play back the comms recording of Gaggenow's last message,' said Harry.

'Dave? Who is Dave,' said the Vizier, looking around – but thankfully not up – suspiciously.

'The computer,' said Harry quickly. 'Just the computer, your Excellency.'

'You have a computer called Dave?'

'Well, yes,' said Harry.

'Replaying message,' said Dave.

A holographic monitor appeared in the air, and began to play back Gaggenow's last message, the one where he was escaping in the *Greene One*, holding the Starheart in his hand, and taunting Tiny Tin.

Then Dave played back a recording of Tiny Tin chasing after him.

'See?' said Barl. 'My mum is telling truth, like always. Now you go, or Barl smash you!'

The Vizier stared at Barl for a moment. 'You're the son of this peculiar creature?' said the Vizier, pointing at Harry.

'Yeah, I am,' said Barl. 'It complicated.'

The Vizier looked Harry up and down. 'Weirdest captain I've ever met. Nice suit, though. Hmm... One last time – have you got the Starheart?'

'No, I just showed you that I haven't!'

'OK, I believe that's what you think, so you're no use to me. Still...you know too much...'

'What?' said Harry. 'I don't know anything!'

'Sorry, can't take that chance. Kill them, kill them all now!' said Plodington Plods.

And the twins released the crates of Canusium metal. They plummeted to the ground, striking their targets perfectly. Both of the Guardians were slammed into the floor with massive force, but they still managed to get a couple of shots off on their way down.

One singed Harry's hand, but not seriously. The other blew a chunk out of one of Barl's legs and he roared in pain.

'Barl,' shouted Harry, horrified.

But then the crates began to move. The Guardians' power armour had saved them from taking any serious damage and they were starting to get up!

'Get out of there, now!' screamed the twins, as they ran along the gantry to the upper exit.

'Yes, come on, Harry, Barl, we've got to move!' yelled Werdle.

Harry helped Barl along, as he limped for the doorway. One of his legs was badly hurt, but at least he had three of them, so it wasn't as bad as it could have been if he'd been human.

'Up, you fools, up,' screamed the Vizier, 'and kill them!'

Harry and his friends reached the door and stepped into the corridor beyond. Behind them, the Guardians rose up in their cybernetic armour with a powered hum, throwing off the crates. Werdle hit the door button, and it slid shut. Then she ripped out some circuits.

'There, sealed shut,' she said. 'Come on!' and they hurried on down the corridor.

'Blast that door open!' shrieked the Vizier from the other side.

'The door won't hold them for more than a minute or two, Captain,' said Dave the computer. 'It's not designed to resist plasma rifles.'

'Got it, thanks, Dave,' said Harry.

As if to underline the computer's words, there was

a sudden blast behind them. The door buckled, but held. For now. Barl, Harry and Werdle reached the end of the corridor, where it formed a T-junction. The twins were waiting for them.

'What are'

'those things?' they said.

'Greys,' said Werdle. 'Super-assassin clones. We breed them for the Imperium. Then they take 'em and enhance them with cybertech – they'll be blindly loyal to whoever they're assigned to.'

'Well done, by the way,' said Harry to the twins. 'That was inspired!'

There was another blast from down the corridor.

'Thanks, Captain, but'

'what do we do now?'

'We can't run for ever!' said the twins.

Barl looked behind. 'Barl fight, maybe, but I think they win,' he said.

'Yeah, you can't fight against plasma rifles,' agreed Harry.

'Captain, what do we do?' said Werdle.

Harry blinked. There was another shattering blast and the door blew apart. Harry stared at a control panel next to him on the wall, and grinned.

'Remember when we first met?' said Harry to the twins.

'This isn't the time for a trip down memory lane!' said Werdle, as the two Guardians began to stomp down the corridor, Plodington Plods close behind.

'Wait a minute,'

'the gravity tiles!' exclaimed the twins, and they laughed.

The *Fartface's* corridors were covered in gravity tiles, which could be adjusted individually. The twins had used this function once to leave Harry floating in the air, with no gravity.

Harry turned to the control panel, and ripped it open. Inside were a set of letters and numbers in Grey, various buttons, and a sliding scale lever. Harry didn't have time to be precise, so he just shoved the lever to

the maximum in a random direction...

And unleashed a superheavy crushing gravity field in the corridor – in fact, in all the corridors all over the ship. Everyone was sent sprawling to the ground.

'Stupid Earth boy!' said the twins through gritted teeth as they hugged the floor, barely able to breathe, let alone move.

'Errk...arg, ferrk...' was all Werdle could say.

'Wrong gravity setting...sorry,' mumbled Harry.

He managed to raise his head and look down the corridor to the cargo bay. The Guardians couldn't move either – in fact, their heavy exoskeletons were now a serious disadvantage. The Grey cloned assassins were bred for speed, not strength. They got that from the suit. But now it was superheavy. And the Vizier was flat on the ground too.

'Urkkle... Smerk... Gak...' was all the Vizier could say.

Harry turned his head. The Guardians were silent, as ever. One was trying to get a hand to a control panel on its suit. That would not be good...

Barl, though, was getting to his feet. He was born on a planet with superheavy gravity. It was what his race was evolved for, so it wasn't nearly so bad for him.

Of course, thought Harry. Maybe he hadn't got the wrong setting, after all!

Harry grinned. 'Go get 'em, Barl,' he said. Harry glanced at the twins. He'd have to pretend this was his idea from the start, rather than just being a bit of luck, of course.

'Be my pleasure, Mum!' said Barl. 'I crush their skulls!'

'No! No. Don't kill them, Barl,' said Harry. 'I mean, they deserve it...but...you know.'

'Not to mention'

'killing the Vizier'

'of the empire'

'that rules the galaxy'

'may attract a'

'little too much attention,' ground out the twins.

'Good point,' hissed Harry through his teeth.

Barl rose up and limped down the corridor. The Guardians and the Vizier were powerless to do anything. They couldn't even speak. Barl, working through the pain his leg was causing him, stripped them of all their gear, tied them up, put them into three empty Canusium crates and sealed them inside, with a few air holes so they could breathe.

Then he set the gravity back to normal.

'Right,' said Harry, getting to his feet. 'We've got to get as far away from here as we can, as fast as we can! Get Barl into med bay, fix that leg with the AutoDoc, Dave – no regeneration, though! Werdle, charge up the quantum drive – we've got to make a jump, now. At the last minute, we'll dump the crates with the bad guys in on the spaceport wharf, and then Dave can seal the hull breach with the force field again, and off we go, before they can do a thing!'

'What about Colum?' said the twins.

'She gone,' said Barl. 'I think maybe she reform while we fight and then make run for it.'

'I don't blame her!' said Harry. 'Let's go!'

An hour later, the *Fartface Banana Nose* was heading out into deep space. Harry was sitting in the captain's chair, with the twins, Barl and Werdle all on station. They were discussing their next move when the computer interrupted them.

'Incoming message,' said Dave.

'What is it?' said Harry.

'Galmail, from Colum – look, I'll put it up on a holographic monitor.'

The message appeared on screen.

Captain Harry.

Thanks again for bailing me out, and don't worry too much. I'm basically OK, though it's going to take a while for me to rearrange my stones in the right order. Anyway, something stinks here, and it stinks badly. I'm not sure what's going on, but I will tell you what I know. My friend Arminius Armpitbreath was exploring the far reaches of the galaxy when he discovered a wrecked Umbonian military scout ship, U-Starboat 653 or something. He found the captain's hat, a big, round steel mushroom thing, inside which was the ship's log. Turns out the Umbonians know something about the Crown Starheart that we didn't. Well, we ordinary citizens, anyway.

If you've seen the Starheart, you'll know that if you look deeply into it, you can see what looks like a tiny galaxy of stars and planets and stuff inside. Sounds pretty, eh?

Turns out it's not just a bunch of pretty lights. It's actually a computerised record of all the military ships and bases in the Hub. If you were an enemy empire – and the Umbonians could well be – you can imagine how valuable that info would be.

So, being a loyal citizen of the Hub, I passed the info on to the Vizier's office. What happened? I got arrested... Go figure. Fortunately, the law – or what's left of it – required that a bail price be posted.

Anyway, I've had enough, it's too dangerous for me! I'm going to go home and pretend to be a pile of rocks for a few months until all this blows over.

Good luck and fibbledibblewibble the porgle poo[26].

Colum
PS Something tells me I probably won't see you ever again. So I'll thank you one last time. Burps.[27]

'Crumbs, I think we may be in over our heads!' said Harry.

---

26. The literal meaning is: 'Don't put chilli powder where the loo roll should be'. Translated as 'take care'.
27. Caryatid for 'thanks'.

'Sounds like we should'

'go and hide out somewhere too,' said the twins, glumly.

'I agree,' said Werdle, 'we need to lie low for a while until things calm down a bit.'

'Where, though?' said Barl.

'Well, actually... I think I've got the perfect place,' said Harry.

21 ALIEN STAKEOUT

THE *Fartface Banana Nose* dropped out of quantum space and into Earth's orbit.

Finally, home at last, after all this time, thought Harry, as he sat in the captain's chair on the bridge.

He looked over at the twins – Bet on the shields station, Alph on propulsion. They'd finally been persuaded that a visit to Earth made sense, as it was a good place to hide from the Vizier, the Leptira, Tiny

Tin, Squeaker Longstockings and anyone else that might be after them. After all, Earth really was in a backwater area of the galaxy that only explorers and fugitives ever visited. They didn't have the Starheart any more, they weren't involved in the issues with that. Even if they had wanted to be involved, what could they do? Gaggenow had fled somewhere with the Starheart, Colum had gone into hiding, Tiny Tin was chasing Gaggenow, and the last people they wanted to see were Clypeus and the Vizier! No, Werdle and the twins had been right – it was best to stay out of it. And once things had calmed down a bit, they'd be able to go back to 'civilisation' (as the others thought of it), but for now this was probably one of the safest places to be. And at the same time Harry could see his mum, let her know he was OK and tell her about his incredible adventures in space.

Werdle was on the sensors station, Barl on weapons. They didn't expect any trouble, of course, but now that Harry had something that could be called a crew, it was best to be prepared. You never know what might come up next, especially when you were... Harry coughed self-consciously, and grinned to himself. Well, when you were a starship captain. He smoothed down his uber-cool, captain's jacket and tugged his cap down a little tighter on his head. He'd have to design a cap badge and everything. But then he lost the grin. What would it be? A face with a banana for a nose? A fart cloud?

He put a hand up to his chin. Well, it could be green, for a start. But then he could feel the bony end of his Grey finger hanging down his chin. A banana, a fart and a grey alien finger on a green background...

Harry sighed.

Werdle frowned. 'Captain, I'm getting some readings,' she said.

'What do you mean?' said Harry.

'Looks like there are at least four other spacecraft orbiting the planet,' she said.

'Probably Earth satellites or the space station,' said Harry.

'My stars, no! These aren't readings of your

primitive satellites or the Meccano set that you call the space station.'

This caused the twins to laugh uproariously. Harry shifted uncomfortably in his chair.

Werdle continued. 'No, these are readings from highly sophisticated ships. 'Wait...err...possibly.'

'Possibly?' said Harry.

'Could be interference of some kind, actually,' said Werdle. 'The readings are faint. Or it could just be that they're on the other side of the planet, or deliberately trying to hide themselves.'

'Are they doing anything?' said Harry.

'No...they seem to be stationary,' said Werdle.

'Hmm...well, let's take a closer look – in the northern hemisphere of the planet, in the continent of Europe, England, Croydon. My home, specifically. We can do that, yes?' said Harry.

'Oh yes, we've got all the abduction protocols and supporting tech. It's what we do...err...did! Once. Umm... Abductions, and that,' said Werdle, her voice tailing off as she looked over at Harry, embarrassed.

But Harry was too interested in the tech to bother

getting annoyed all over again at what the Greys had done to him.

'So, how does it work?'

'Simple, really. It's a camouflaged stealth drone, bristling with superadvanced camera tech. We send it down to snoop around,' said Werdle.

'OK, display on the holographic monitor,' said Harry.

Up came his road. Coalsack Lane. There it was, just the same as always! Cars going up and down the street; two traffic wardens; people waiting for the number 14 bus into town; the Taste More cafe, the Sultan's Kebab House, the Royal Oak pub, and Coal's Corner shop, still there, as if nothing had happened. And at the end of the street – Coalsack Secondary School. There, walking to school, were Todd Scarswell and his gang! They'd made his life a misery at school. But now they seemed – well, a minor irritation, really. Once you'd escaped from a Leptiran pie in which you were the main ingredient, or fought a duel almost to the death on a dust-covered alien planet, having someone laugh at the playlists on your MP3 player really didn't amount to much, did it?

And who was that skulking behind them, trying not to draw Todd's attention? Harvey! Harry's mate from the next-door flat. Boy, would he love to hear about Harry's adventures. And he'd laugh and laugh when he found out it was all down to him that the *Fartface Banana Nose* was called...well, the *Fartface Banana Nose*!

The view zoomed in – Theseus House, the council estate where Harry lived, just the same as it ever was, a great big block of dirty grey stone with dirty grey walls, dirty grey floors, dirty grey stairs leading up to four dirty grey levels. A little tear sprang up in Harry's eye at the sight of it. Home!

'Eurgh, what a'

'truly revolting'

'dump!' said the twins.

Harry's tears dried up in an instant, and his head sank back against his chair. Trust the twins to bring him back down to Earth (literally...hah, hah!)

He sighed. They were probably right, though – it was a bit of a dump.

'Really? We thought that had to be some kind of high status place, what with it being so beautifully grey and square,' said Werdle.

The twins began to screech with laughter. Harry shook his head.

The view closed in further – at the front was a kids' playground. He'd spent many an hour on those swings with Harvey in times gone by. Behind the playground was the main entrance to the flats, and just inside that on the left was their first floor flat where his mum would be. Harvey's flat was next door to that. Harry's mum was probably sitting at the kitchen table, getting ready for work, drinking that horrible tea she loved – what was it called? Oh yes, Lapsang Souchong. It sounded more like someone – something, rather – he might have met recently than a tea! Maybe he'd join her for a cup and some toast. Soon, hopefully. How wonderful that would be!

'Hold on, Captain...is that...? My stars, look at that!' said Werdle.

On the roof of Theseus House a figure was leaning out and peering down at the entrance – a red-furred, three-legged, barrel-chested figure, wearing yellow stockings patterned with purple polka dots. One side of her face was covered in some kind of metal plate, and she was holding a blaster rifle, with a sniper scope.

'Squeaker Longstockings!' said Barl and Harry together.

'How'd she...' muttered Harry. Then he noticed something else – across the street, some kind of supermarket delivery van, parked up. It said 'Painsbury's Pies' on the side. He'd never heard of it.

'Can you see inside that van?' said Harry.

'Yes, hold on, we've got digitally enhanced deep vision cameras,' said Werdle.

The walls of the van began to dissolve away on the screen to reveal...three Leptira! They were dressed in obviously fake supermarket uniforms with little supermarket caps and...beards! False beards!

Harry laughed out loud. The Leptira were hopeless at disguises. But the laughter died on his lips. Bad at disguises they may be, but it still meant that there were man-eating alien insects on the

243

streets of Croydon, just yards away from his mum.

Then he noticed something popping up from a manhole cover, on the same side of the street. Werdle noticed too and zoomed in. It was a periscope, peeping up every now and again, taking a look around, then dropping back down.

'Wha...?' stuttered an astonished Harry. 'Can we get a look down there?'

'Sure thing, Captain,' said Werdle. 'Enhancing camera for poor light conditions.'

The drone revealed...

Tiny Tin – hiding in a manhole, a periscope coming out of the top of his head, spying on Theseus House.

They were all there, staking out Harry's mum's flat, waiting for him to turn up! But why? Gaggenow had the Starheart – it didn't make sense. Unless

Gaggenow was visiting Harry's mum? No, that was ridiculous. Then...they must think Harry had the Starheart after all! It had to be that. Gaggenow must have pulled a fast one – he'd probably convinced them Harry had it, and told them all about his mum, to save his own skin, the clown-footed little...

'I'll bet the Vizier and his Guardian goons are somewhere around as well,' said Werdle.

The thought chilled Harry to the bone. 'Can we find them?' said Harry.

'Probably not. They'll have advanced Hub tech to hide behind,' said Werdle. 'Still scanning, though.'

'Wait a minute, what about those three there?' said Harry. 'Sitting outside the Taste More cafe.'

'What about them?' said Werdle. 'They look human.'

'Yeah, but look what they've ordered. An enormous mound of toast. And one of them's sprinkling something on a slice. Look, it's green and glittery. Grerk spice!'

'But they're human,' said Werdle.

'Holo-harnesses, I bet,' said Harry. 'When we first met Gaggenow he looked human too, disguised by one of those things.'

'Until Harry'

'broke it,'

'that is,' said the twins.

'Could be a harness, good point,' said Werdle. 'Let's take a closer look. Look, there! See, isn't that a bit of white fur on the back of its neck, poking through the holographic disguise? It's Plodington Plods, I'll bet!'

'Why's he there on his own?' said Harry. 'Why doesn't he send some kind of Hub spy team or something? Why just him and his two goons?'

'Don't know, it strange,' said Barl.

'Maybe he's here "unofficially", as it were,' said Werdle.

'Well, either way,

'it looks like'

'we can't possibly'

'stay here after all.'

'Oh, what a shame!' the twins finished sarcastically.

'But I have to see my mum! After all this, I've got to let her know I'm alive and well,' said Harry.

'Tricky...' said Barl.

'And then we'll have to get out of here,' said Harry.

'OK by us!' said the twins.

'Except...'

'What?' said the twins.

'We have to let that lot know we're leaving,' said Harry, 'so they chase us.'

'WHAT?' said the twins.

'To get them away from here. From my mum, my mate Harvey, the school. All right, Todd Scarswell and his mates aren't exactly my favourite people but they don't deserve to get shot with lasers or eaten by aliens, right? Nor do the teachers and the rest of the kids at school, in fact. Well, maybe Miss Turner. She seemed to spend most of her time giving me detention, but still...' said Harry.

'Are they in'

'that much danger?' said the twins.

'What, surrounded by a deadly hunter robot, some hungry flesh-eating aliens, the second most powerful being in the galaxy who appears to have gone mad, and a homicidal maniac who lives only for revenge? They'd kidnap my mum just to get at me, no trouble! Yeah, I think they're in danger!'

'Well, when you'

'put it like that.'

'I know it's a lot to ask, but I need you all to help me protect my mum. It'll be risky, but...will you?'

'What if we simply took her with us?' said Werdle.

Harry shook his head. 'I've thought about that but it wouldn't be fair. She's got a life and friends and everything here. Plus it's far too dangerous out in the galaxy,' said Harry. 'She could get marooned on a planet, or shot out of space, or end up in a Leptiran recipe book!'

'Fair point,' said Werdle.

'No, I need your help to get me in there and out again. Will you?'

'Barl help you and Grandma, course,' said Barl.

'Hey, it's my job, you pay me for this,' said Werdle. 'I'm in.'

The twins looked at each other and then back at Harry.

'Well, we think'

'you've been a good captain'

'even though your manners'

'leave something to be desired,'

'so we'll help too,' said the twins.

Harry smiled back at them.

'Also...' added Bet, 'we kind of like you.'

Alph folder her arms. 'S'pose,' she said.

'Cool, thanks!' said Harry. 'I like you too!' Again, Harry felt a tear welling up. He really did like them, they were so blue and golden and...

'Well, of course you do,'

'who wouldn't?'

'That's a given,' said the twins.

The tear dried up like a drop of water on the outside hull of a Tricrusian tracker ship during a Sundrive jump.

'**SO,** no one's seen my Survivor 2000 Packhorse backpack?' asked Harry.

'For the hundredth time, no!' said Werdle.

'Sorry, Mum, no,' said Barl.

'What would we'

'possibly want'

'with such a thing?' said the twins.

'I'm afraid not, Captain,' added Dave the computer.

Harry sighed. His backpack had his water dispenser and his phone in it, but he couldn't find the blasted thing anywhere. It was annoying because although the phone's battery had died, it wasn't exactly complicated tech compared to Hub stuff, and Werdle was an engineer. She could probably have got it charged up and then he could have phoned his mum – told her to meet him somewhere or something. Thankfully he now wore his Survivor 2000 Multi-Knife on his belt, or he'd have lost that too, he thought, as he put a hand on the matt-black cylinder at his side.

He shook his head. He remembered transferring the pack from the *Greene One* to the *Fartface*, with the rest of his stuff but where had he put it?

'I'm sorry you've lost it. We'll just have to manage without it. So let's tell everyone the plan, OK, Harry?' said Werdle.

'Right. Well, we go in at night – it's simply impossible to go in during the day, as the street will be full of people and cars and stuff. About one in the morning (local time) sounds good,' said Harry.

Werdle took it from there: 'Alph and Bet will put down a pair of holo-vid generators at the far end of the street. Turn them on – that'll bring up a couple of holograms of Barl and Harry heading away from Theseus House. Hopefully it'll distract the various parties involved long enough for the real Barl and Harry to get in and see Harry's mum.'

'How are we all going to get down there?' said the twins.

'The Abduction Ray. It's a modified Gravitronic

Grappler – we use it to pick up specimens...err... people, I mean! To pick up and put down people on the surface of planets,' said Werdle.

'Doesn't that mean the *Fartface* has to go into the atmosphere, you know, close to the surface?' said Harry.

'Yes, indeed,' said Werdle.

'Hold on,' said Harry. 'Isn't there a chance that the ship might show up on radar and stuff? It'd be a serious UFO sighting, for sure – they might even send up some jets to take a look or something!'

'There's no chance, Harry. Earthling technology simply isn't up to overcoming our stealth systems,' said Werdle. 'No need to worry.'

'No surprise'

'there, then,' said the twins smugly.

'OK, OK,' said Harry, 'I get it. Anyway, on with the plan – Werdle puts the twins down at the far end of the street. They do their stuff. Then Werdle puts me and Barl – I'll need him, in case there's trouble – down at the front entrance of Theseus House. Then Werdle switches the ray, brings the twins back up. Meanwhile I talk to Mum, I come out, Werdle brings us back up, and we jump,' said Harry.

'Sounds like a plan!' said Werdle.

'That's doomed'

'to fail,' finished the twins with a giggle.

'Got a better idea?' said Harry, hands on hips, his squid finger dangling down his upper thigh.

The twins put their heads to one side at the same time, and stared at Harry with their golden eyes. Then they straightened up, and shook their heads in perfect harmony.

'Nope.'

'Sorry. Guess it'

'will have to do,' they said.

'OK, then, let's get ready. We'll meet in the Abduction Ray chamber at 12.30 tonight. Earth time, that is, got it?

'Got it, Captain!' everybody chorused.

Harry nodded his approval, and everyone moved away to make their preparations, leaving Harry alone with his thoughts.

'Won't be long now, Mum,' he said to himself.

'**YOU'RE** going to go'

'dressed like that?' said the twins.

They were standing in the Abduction Ray chamber. The Abduction Ray itself was a twenty foot long, four-tubed column of high tech astonishment – topped with what looked like a great big grey toilet bowl. It was called the 'Gravitronic Emitter'. Harry preferred to call it the toilet bowl.

Harry was standing in front of it, wearing his full dress captain's uniform, the one the twins had bought him.

'I mean, we think'

'it's a great outfit,'

'but it's hardly'

'inconspicuous, is it?' said the twins.

The twins themselves were dressed in dark blue jump suits – stylish, mind, but hard to see at night, so practical too. Each held a suitcase-sized holo-vid generator.

'I just want my mum to see me like this. To see I'm a captain and everything.'

The twins looked at each other.

'Ahhhhh, how sweet...'

'IDIOT!' they said.

'Well, whatever.' Harry shrugged. 'If it goes well, I won't get spotted until after I've seen Mum anyway, and it won't matter then.'

Werdle was sitting inside a cockpit at the back end of the Abduction Ray, in front of a console monitor, as if it were some kind of sophisticated anti-aircraft gun.

'So,' said Werdle, 'the ray will pick you up, enclosing you in an hermetically sealed energy field, where you can breathe safely. Then I'll use the ray to move you down through the atmosphere to the target area.'

'Riiiighht...'

'That sounds'

'perfectly safe,' said the twins.

Harry laughed.

'Don't worry, we won't fill the energy field with

the usual knockout gas,' said Werdle. 'You'll be fine!'

'Great, thanks'

'for that,' said the twins.

'Right, it's time, let's do it – or rather, let's let you guys do it! I'd like to officially thank the stars that only I know how to work the Abductor!' said Werdle.

'Why?' said Harry.

'It's a suici... Err...you know, I don't like all that gung-ho stuff! Much prefer to be a techy. Ahem.' Werdle coughed.

'OK, then, let's go,' said Harry.

Werdle activated the Abductor Ray. The twins were engulfed in a bright, white light, so bright that Harry and Barl had to shield their eyes. The far wall of the chamber opened up to the night sky high above Croydon.

Cold night air rushed into the chamber, carrying the lost smells of Earth to Harry's eager nostrils – that was, old rubber tyres, fresh paint from new double yellow lines, the remnants of recently fried kebabs and chips, the ever present exhaust fumes and stale beer from the pub. It was a welcome smell to Harry after so long away but Barl wrinkled up his nose and coughed.

'Bah! Earth stink!' he said.

Harry looked over at him. What could he say? Then he looked up at the drone monitor. A bright light filled the end of Coalsack Lane, and then it winked out. The twins were deposited gently at the far end, opposite the Royal Oak. They turned up their noses at the beery smell and the cigarette butts piled up outside.

'Yuk, what a stink,'

'Earth schnek schnek noobs,'[28] they said over the comms link.

---

28. Nearest Earth equivalent: 'Earth really sucks'.

'Just get on with it!' said Harry, curtly.

The twins took a few steps past the pub and then placed their holo generators in the darkest part of the street they could find. Then they turned them on and stepped back.

Convincing-looking holograms (well, in the poor light, that was) appeared on the street, walking and talking their way away from Theseus House. Harry, Barl and Werdle looked at the screens, monitoring the stakeout crew – Squeaker had already seen the holograms, and was aiming her blaster rifle!

'Crack! Crack! Crack!' rang out like cannon fire as her scoped blaster rifle fired arrows of deadly energy at the holograms.

Harry's draw dropped. No waiting, no delay, she was prepared to just kill them both as quickly as she possibly could! Wow, she must hate him more than she ever had before.

Then all hell broke loose.

One of the twins – Harry couldn't see which – went down with a cry, shot through the leg by a blaster beam that had passed through a hologram, and ricocheted off the road.

Tiny Tin burst up and out of his manhole cover in an instant, and crouched, at the ready.

The back of the Painsbury's Pies van opened and the three Leptira emerged.

A door opened in the air out of nowhere above the street, and Plodington Plods and his Guardian Commandos began to walk down a seemingly invisible stairway...

'Hub-tech Stealth Car!' said Werdle.

'Alph, Bet, are you OK?' shouted Harry over the comms system.

'Alph...she's...I've got her,' said Bet.

'Get them back, Werdle, now!' said Harry.

'No!' said Bet.

The robot, the Vizier and the Leptira began to advance down the street. Squeaker was adjusting her scope, no doubt puzzled as to why she hadn't put Barl and Harry down already, not yet realising they were holograms.

'Alph's fine,' continued Bet, 'I've got her, we're in the shadows of this horrible smelly place with the funny sign of the hairy human in a tree. You go in, Harry, we'll be fine, otherwise there'll be no time!'

'She's right,' said Werdle, 'the wound doesn't look fatal. Get into place, now. Don't worry, the twins will be back on board and Alph will be in the AutoDoc in a matter of minutes anyway!'

Barl and Harry stepped forward to be bathed in the light of the Abductor Ray.

Meanwhile, two more laser blasts cracked out at the holograms – to no effect, except that one of the Leptira, a little jumpy and thinking they were under fire, shot back at Squeaker's position with a plasma gun, blowing a chunk of the concrete roof off. It clattered to the ground with a roaring crack.

Lights began to go on in the houses on the street.

Harry and Barl were picked up by the ray, shot through the air like parcels in a vacuum tube, and deposited in the stairwell just below Harry's flat. Harry looked up. He pointed to a blue door up ahead. Number 29. Next to it, number 28, was Harvey's place – with a bright pink door. Harvey hated that door. Barl moved up to the blue door, Harry just behind.

'Wait!' said Harry. 'Let me go first. I'll use my key. You should stay outside for a minute or two, otherwise you'll terrify the life out of Mum!'

There was another crack of blaster fire, followed by the rushing whoosh of a Leptiran plasma weapon.

Then the outside light at number 29 came on, and the door opened. Harry's mum looked up into the face of Barl.

'Hi, Grandma!' said Barl.

'**AIIIIEEEEEEEEEEE!**' screamed Harry's mum.

Harry stepped out from behind Barl. 'Mum, it's me, Harry!'

Ariadne Greene, in her late thirties, slim, with tousled blonde hair, wearing a pair of Spider-Man pyjamas, with a cup of Lapsang Souchong tea in her hand, froze in mid-scream.

'Harry? Where have you been? And what in blue blazes are you wearing? And what have you done with your school uniform?' she said. And then it seemed she couldn't believe that was the first thing she'd said after so much time. Or after such a weird dream as she must have been having...or nightmare.

'It's my new uniform, Mum!' said Harry, a huge smile beginning to spread all over his face. 'Mum! I missed you so much!' And he stepped forward to give her a big hug, tears rolling down over his wide smile.

Ariadne hugged him back with all the love a mother could feel for a lost son but then, over his shoulder, she saw again...the big, red-furred, blue-eyed three-legged thing. And it stepped forward to make it into a group hug.

'Good to see family back together,' said Barl.

'Arghhhh! What is it?' screamed Ariadne, extracting herself from the embrace and backing into the flat. 'And why does it smell of curry?'

'Don't worry, Mum. He's my...friend. And he's called Barl. He's from another planet. And he always smells of curry.'

'What?' said Ariadne. She looked from Harry to Barl and back again.

'I got abducted by aliens, Mum. But then...well, I...I'm a captain now. A starship captain. Look!'

And he gave a twirl to show off his new uniform.

'Argghhhh!' screamed Ariadne. 'What's that, on your hand?' She was pointing at Harry's squid finger.

'What? Oh, that, it's—' said Harry.

'You're an alien too! A pod person or something, trying to take over my son's life, aren't you?'

'No, no!' said Harry.

'What have you done with the real Harry, you alien monster!' said Ariadne, stepping forward, fist clenched, cup of tea in her other hand like a weapon, her eyes narrowed in anger, voice full of vengeful fury, just like when she was in full on 'telling him off' mode.

Harry and Barl quailed before her.

'Wait, it's really me!' said Harry. 'I mean, my MP3 player, it's got a playlist you made me, with all those oldies I love, called 'Indiemums Rule', every Christmas we watch *The Lord of the Rings*, we've got a rescue cat called Gollum who's only got one ear, I fell off a swing once and had to have seven stitches, you've also got Thor and Iron Man pyjamas coz you're more of a superhero fan than I am, and... It's

264

me, Mum, and I love you!'

'Harry? Is it really you?' said Ariadne, hope lighting up her face.

'Yes, Mum, it really is and I'm sorry, I can't explain everything, I haven't got time. Here, have this!' Harry gave her a small holo device. 'Press that button – I'll appear in a little 3D video and tell you everything that's happened to me since I went missing.'

'I'm so cross with you, Harry. Why couldn't you at least phone me? We agreed that you'd use that phone to ring me – that's the only reason I let you have one!' said Harry's mum.

'I know, Mum, but there's no signal on the wrong side of the galaxy, and since then I lost it,' said Harry.

'Don't you lie to me, Harry Greene, you...'

'It true, Grandma,' said Barl. 'Harry marooned on my planet on other side of galaxy. And now he a great captain, with own ship and everything!'

Ariadne stared at Barl. They could see her brain working. But all she could get out was, 'Why does it keep calling me Grandma?'

'It's complicated,' said Barl and Harry together.

Suddenly there was a shattering explosion, and the wall blew in, spraying dust and rubble everywhere.

Barl, Ariadne and Harry were covered in dust, like fine white flour. As it settled, they could see a great big gaping hole in the wall that separated them from Harvey's flat. And there were Harvey and his mum and dad, sitting in a row on their couch, tied and gagged, staring at them in wide-eyed horror!

'Harvey...' stuttered Harry. 'What...?'

And then a great big hunk of walking metal filled the hole.

Tiny Tin!

'Sorry, wrong flat,' said Tiny Tin as he stepped into the room and levelled his Deth Ray at Harry.

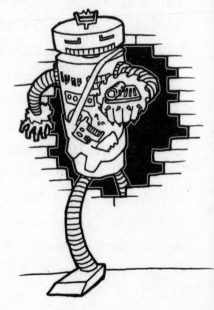

'Got you now, though,' the robot grated.

Ariadne stared, open-mouthed.

Barl tensed, ready to leap, but Tiny Tin aimed his Deth Ray at him and said, 'I've just blown a hole in this wall. Don't think for a moment I won't do the same to you!'

'Don't, Barl, don't get yourself killed,' said Harry.

Barl growled, but didn't move. He knew Harry was right. Tiny Tin had them trapped.

Tiny Tin moved into the room. 'You're coming with me, Captain Greene,' said the robot.

'Never!' said Harry.

'Oh, really?' said Tiny Tin, turning to point the Deth Ray at Harry's mum. Ariadne, covered in white dust from head to foot, cup of tea still in her hand, shrank back. All she could manage was a plaintive squeak of terror.

'All right, all right, you've got me!' said Harry. 'Just don't hurt my mum!'

Tiny Tin turned back to Harry.

'Good.' He motioned to the door with his Deth Ray. 'Let's go,' rattled the robot.

But then Ariadne stepped up behind the robot, reached up and...poured her tea into a small vent on the robot's back.

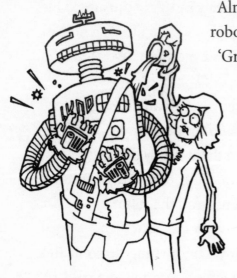

Almost immediately the robot jerked to attention. 'Grrkk..unknown liquid in cooling system,' crackled the robot and it began to shake and rattle. Sparks started to fizz and fly. 'Cannot metabolise liquid... Major system failure... Shorting out...' said the robot.

'Yeah, I hate Lapsang Souchong too!' said Harry.

Ariadne stepped back as Tiny Tin froze up completely. Then the robot toppled to the ground with a crash where it lay, sparking, fizzing, whirring and hissing.

'No one points a Deth Ray at my son!' said Ariadne. 'Least of all an eight-foot tin robot who can't spell.'

'Way to go, Grandma!' said Barl.

'Wow, thanks, Mum,' said Harry. 'You beat Tiny

268

Tin! He's one of the most bad-ass bounty hunters in the whole galaxy!'

Ariadne scowled. 'Bounty hunter? What did you do, Harry? Did you break the law?'

'No...no! Ummm...well...I mean...'

'Harry?' said Mum, folding her arms.

'It's a long story, Mum, honest, Mum, it wasn't my fault.'

Behind them, in the next flat, Harvey and his mum and dad, still tied to the couch and gagged, stared and stared – at Harry in a captain's suit, at Ariadne in her Spider-Man pyjamas, at the enormous three-legged, red-furred alien, all of them covered in white dust, and at the huge robot at their feet, twitching and sparking.

And then something began to move on the robot's chest. A hatch! A hatch was lifting up!

Harry, Barl and Ariadne stepped back. A tiny figure pulled itself up and out of the sparking robot – a small humanoid alien, no more than a foot high, with thin, spindly legs and arms, and a big head. It looked a bit like a gremlin – a very thin, hairless, dirty-brown-coloured gremlin with

big floppy ears and black shades.
Techy black shades.

(Behind them, in the next
room, Harvey's mum's eyes
rolled up into her head and
she passed out.)

'You're Tiny Tin?' said
Harry, mouth agape.

'Yeah,' chirped the
little alien, 'I'm Tiny Tin.'

'You're the most bad-ass
bounty hunter in the galaxy?' said Ariadne.

'YEAH! I am, just deal with it, OK?' said Tiny
Tin belligerently.

'Hah, hah,' said Barl, 'you just little thing!'

Tiny Tin glared up at Barl. 'Yeah, well, this little
thing kicked your ass back on Haddus, remember?'
he said, angrily.

Barl folded his arms. 'Things a bit different now,
though, aren't they?' he said lifting up a foot.

Tiny Tin looked up at him and gulped.

'All right! All right, Barl, there's no need for that,'
said Harry. 'OK, he's caused us a lot of trouble, but

to be fair, he never actually hurt us or killed anyone, right?'

'If count knocking me out with hypodermic not hurting anyone,' said Barl.

'Well, sorry about that, but it could have been worse, couldn't it? I mean, I never used my Deth Ray on anyone,' said Tiny Tin.

Harry's mum was staring at the little creature in amazement. 'Where are you from?' she said automatically.

'Planet called Woggle,' said Tiny. 'They call us Wogglers.'

'Wogglers? Hah, hah!' said Harry. 'Wogglers!'

'Laugh all you like, alien freak,' said Tiny Tin, 'but Woggle means Big Tech in our language, and we're the best robotic engineers in the galaxy!'

'Well, as you're visiting, would you like a cup of tea?' said Harry's mum, still without thinking.

Tiny Tin looked up at her. 'No. No thanks.'

'What are we going to do with you?' said Harry.

'Nothing,' said Tiny Tin, 'I'm leaving.' With that, he reached over to a button on the robot's head and pressed it. The head detached itself and rolled over, forming a kind of bucket, into which Tiny Tin began to climb.

'Hey, maybe we just smash you or take you prisoner!' said Barl.

'Yeah, maybe, or you could just let me go,' said Tiny Tin as he positioned himself inside the robot's head. 'I think you'll let me go,' continued Tiny Tin as he hit another control somewhere inside the head. 'Your captain isn't the killing sort, and I'll be more trouble than I'm worth to take with you.'

Three spindly robotic spider legs suddenly sprouted out of the sides of the head, and it rose up on them – a robotic spider head with a tiny rider inside it.

(Behind them, on the couch, Harvey's dad's eyes rolled up into his head and he passed out. Harvey was made of tougher stuff, though – he was staring in fascinated amazement. Harry could almost see him thinking: *Best computer game graphics ever!*)

'But you just come after us again,' said Barl, stepping forward.

'You'll be long gone by the time I fix myself up another robot body,' said Tiny Tin, as he scuttled forward on his robot-head spider chariot.

'Why are you after me anyway, don't you want Gaggenow?' said Harry.

Tiny Tin stared up at Harry for a moment. 'You actually don't know, do you? Well, whatever, I really must be going. If you don't mind?' Tiny Tin looked up at Barl who was blocking the doorway.

'Might as well let him go, I suppose,' said Harry.

'OK, see ya, then,' said Tiny Tin who scuttled away through Barl's legs and out of the door as fast as he could before Harry could change his mind.

Outside, the sound of police sirens filled the night.

Harry looked over at his mum. He smiled sadly at her.

'We've got to go as well, I'm afraid,' said Harry.

'You're not going to stay?' said Ariadne.

'I can't, Mum. I know it's weird, but I'm kind of... well, important, I guess. I've got a crew, and stuff, and a mission. An important mission!'

'You can't even stay for a cup of tea?' said Ariadne.

A flash of light from outside filled the room, followed by a booming crash – more energy weapons being discharged. They'd dealt with Tiny Tin, but the Vizier and the Leptira were still out there. Harry dreaded to think what would happen if they got here!

'Come, we must go,' said Barl.

'Sorry, Mum. Goodbye! I promise I'll be in touch, soon!'

Harry looked over at Harvey who was staring back at him with wild eyes. He waved. 'See you, Harvey. Sorry, mate, gotta go. Mum'll untie you, I'm sure.'

With that, he turned for the door. His mum stared after him, lifted a solitary hand, looking dazed and confused.

'Mmm...grrkkkk...arrrrk...' moaned Harvey.

HARRY ran down the stairs, Barl just behind him.

'Now, Werdle! Activate ray,' said Barl into his comms ear piece.

The stairwell filled with a bright light, and Barl and Harry were swept up into the Abductor Ray like leaves on the wind. Seconds later, they were back on the bridge of the *Fartface*.

'Dave, how's Alph doing?' said Harry.

'OK,' said Dave the computer. 'She's in the med bay already.'

'What's happening with the Vizier and the rest?' said Harry.

'They've clocked the Abductor Ray, they know what's going on. Looks like they're all boarding their ships, and coming after us. A Tricrusian tracker, a Leptiran battle cruiser, and the personal space yacht of the Imperial Vizier, Plodington Plods. No bounty hunter stealth ship, though...'

'Yeah, Tiny Tin, errr...he's having a tea break,' said Harry.

'Well, either way you're certainly attracting a lot of attention!' said Dave.

Harry made a face. 'I'm going to see how the twins are doing,' he said. 'Werdle, you handle the jump with Dave, we've got to go, as soon as!'

'Yes, Captain – but what's with all that white dust you're covered in? Looks like you've been baking bread – really badly!' said Werdle.

Before Harry could answer, Dave interjected. 'Hold on,' said the computer, 'I'm getting...there's someone...seems like we've got an intruder! In your cabin!'

'What!' said Harry? 'How?'

'I don't know,' said Dave. 'It's using some kind of sensor dampening field.'

'Right,' said Harry, 'Barl, with me! Werdle, get that quantum drive up!'

Harry and Barl rushed off. A minute or two later and they were approaching the Captain's Cabin, Harry with his sword at the ready, Barl right behind him. The door to the Captain's Cabin swished open...

At the far end, a figure was going through Harry's cupboard.

'Hey, you! Stop!' bellowed Barl.

The figure turned. It was carrying something in one hand.

'GAGGENOW!' shouted Harry.

Gaggenow blinked at them in surprise, one hand waving as if trying to brush something away, his head bobbing downwards in a classic gesture of red-handed guilt.

'What are you doing, you little sneak?' said Harry.

'Errr...looking for...a snack!' babbled Gaggenow.

'Oh, come on...' said Harry, in exasperation.

'I like the suit, Harry, very nice,' said Gaggenow with an ingratiating grin. He tried to salute with one hand, but he was holding Harry's backpack, so he saluted with the other. 'But what's with all the flour?'

'Don't change the subject – and that's my backpack! I should have known you'd stolen it,' said Harry.

'Actually, technically that is incorrect. In fact, I hid it at the back of your cupboard, under a grav panel,' said Gaggenow.

'What? Why?' said Harry, stepping closer, sword at the ready. Gaggenow gulped at the sight of it. He'd seen what Harry could do with it.

'Well, it was such an ugly thing, I thought you'd prefer it if I—' And then suddenly Gaggenow's face fell. His shoulders fell. His body fell – to his many jointed knees on the floor.

'Oh, what's the use?' he bleated. 'I just can't take it any more, I just can't take it!' Gaggenow put his hands over his eyes and sobbed.

Harry turned off his sword. He looked up at Barl, and back at Gaggenow.

'Watch out,' whispered Barl, 'probably another trick.'

Harry nodded. 'What's with the backpack, Gaggenow?' he said.

'I put the Starheart inside, and hid it,' said Gaggenow.

'What? I saw you fly off with that, in the Tracker – which saved us, by the way, so thanks for that. Which is why I haven't thrown you into a holding cell already, I might add!'

'Hah, I wasn't saving you,' said Gaggenow, looking up, his eyes red with milky white tears, 'I was saving myself. Well, perhaps both of us, to be fair – but that was by accident.'

'What do you mean?' said Harry.

'I went off with a fake Starheart, you see,' whimpered Gaggenow.

'Fake?' said Barl, in astonished tones.

'Yeah. Made out of boiled sugar. 'Fraid I've eaten it. There's none left, sorry.'

'And you hid the real one in my cabin?' said Harry.

'Yes. Once they'd found out the one I had was fake, they went back to looking for you,' said Gaggenow, 'instead of me.'

'Ah, I see,' said Harry, folding his arms.

'I knew you'd find where Earth was. I mean, you are amazing, Harry, amazing! All the stuff you've done, like rescuing us from the Leptira. Even fighting one face to face. Incredible!'

Harry frowned. Gaggenow never complimented him. Ever. And he was talking as he never had talked. Maybe this time, for the first time, he was actually telling the truth. Maybe he really had had enough. It wouldn't be that surprising, after all. He must have been under a massive strain, all this time, being chased from one side of the galaxy to the other.

Gaggenow went on in a rush. 'So, yes. I knew you would find Earth. And then you'd go and see your mum. And whilst you were visiting, I'd steal back the Starheart and be on my way, while everyone else would still be looking for you and not me.'

'Clever. Cunning little swindler you are,' said Barl.

'Thank you,' said Gaggenow absently. 'But what I

didn't figure on is the rest of them working out that you'd want to go home too. I mean, none of them have ever heard of Earth before! I nearly gave up on the whole thing when I saw them arrive. But what could I do? I knew you were clever enough to get in and out without being caught. And I had to try it.'

'Why, though? I mean all this...just in case the Vizier gives you back your family? Or are you working for the Umbonians or something? Is that it?' said Harry.

Gaggenow blinked up at him, the colour draining from his already pale face, to leave it chalky white, as if it were the face of fear itself.

'So, you know! You know what the Starheart really is?' said Gaggenow.

'Yes, I know. It's vital to the defence of the empire,' said Harry. 'Are you going to sell it to the Umbonians, is that it?'

'No, no! I... Don't you see?'

'No,' said Harry. 'Tell me!'

'It's the Vizier. Plodington Plods himself. He made me do it,' said Gaggenow.

'Why?' said Harry.

'He's the one who's in cahoots with the Umbonian League. He's promised to give them the Starheart. In return, once they've conquered the Hub, they'll make him the governor, a puppet ruler under the Umbonians but a ruler nevertheless,' said Gaggenow.

'Wow!' muttered Harry. 'Just wow!'

'And then the Umbonians would make us all wear the Hat of Utter Submission,' sighed Gaggenow miserably.

'Hah, they've promised to make me wear the Hat of Crawling Worminess!' said Harry.

Gaggenow looked up at him. 'Farglian fudge, Harry, isn't there anyone in the galaxy you haven't annoyed?'

'Hah, certainly feels like the whole galaxy is against me sometimes,' said Harry.

'I know how you feel,' said Gaggenow.

It was all beginning to make sense, thought Harry to himself. That's why the Vizier was going around on his own – it was just him and his two goons who were in on it. He couldn't let anyone else know, and that's why he wanted to kill Colum, and Harry, and all his crew. So, in that case...

'Why don't you hand over the Starheart to the Galactic Overlord himself?' said Harry.

'Tricky. Very hard to see the overlord, very hard. Usually you have to get permission from – you guessed it – the Vizier! And anyway. Plodington Plods has my family,' said Gaggenow.

'I thought you didn't want them back?' said Harry.

'Bah,' said Gaggenow waving a hand dismissively. 'That was just bravado. Bluff. To be honest, I'm not that bothered about half of them but...'

'But?' said Harry.

'My mother,' said Gaggenow. 'I love my mother. I know it's a weakness, but I had to try to save her. And also...well, try to prevent the Starheart falling into the hands of the Umbonians.'

Harry stood there for a moment, arms folded. He knew how Gaggenow felt again.

'How do you know that the Vizier hasn't already killed them because you didn't hand the Starheart over?' asked Harry.

'I...I don't, not for sure. But I don't think he

would, not now that I have the Starheart. If he does, he knows I'd never give it to him then. It's a bit of a...'

'Mexican standoff?'

'Whatever. Anyway, I have had enough, Harry. Enough. I can't do it any more,' said Gaggenow, 'I just can't. I'm sorry!' and his tears turned into wracking sobs.

Harry made a face. He wanted to comfort Gaggenow, put an arm around him, tell him it would be all right. But he also wanted to put him in a Haddusian blow cart with broken brakes, or a Leptiran pie, or maroon him on a planet with really, really heavy gravity or...argh, so many things!

He sighed, and raised his eyes. But if it was true, all that Gaggenow had been saying, he couldn't really blame him. If it was all true, that was... But then again...it all seemed so convincing!

'You've got to help me, Harry, please!' said Gaggenow.

'Me! Why would I? More to the point, *how* could I?' said Harry.

'Ahh...well,' said Gaggenow. He stared at

Harry for a second or two.

'Well?' said Harry.

'You've proved yourself to be very resourceful, haven't you? A captain, a fighter, a tactician, a leader. All that stuff.'

'Stop buttering me up and get to the point!' said Harry.

'You have to help me get in front of the Galactic Overlord and rescue my family,' said Gaggenow with a rush of words.

Harry blinked at him. Rescue his... From the Vizier? Get him in front...of the overlord of the galaxy? How on Earth (or wherever) was he supposed to do all that?

Gaggenow looked at him expectantly.

Harry looked back.

'It's the only way to get everyone who's after us off our backs – yours as well as mine!' said Gaggenow.

'But it's all your fault they're after me in the first place!' said Harry.

Gaggenow shrugged. 'We are where we are,' he said.

Harry frowned. That was true, punishing

285

Gaggenow for it was like crying over spilled milk. Or crying over spilled Farglian roach pus.

'Well, what do you say?' said Gaggenow.

'You really think I can do those things?' said Harry.

Gaggenow nodded. 'Yes, of course. You fought a space battle with a Leptiran battle cruiser, and lived. You sneaked aboard the very same Leptiran battle cruiser, got all the prisoners off. You outwitted the Vizier, the Vizier of the whole empire! Not to mention dealing with Squeaker wotsit, that crazy Tricrusian – sorry Barl, no offence.'

'None taken.' Barl shrugged.

'Escaped from a planet you'd been marooned on with nothing but a knife and a water dispenser. And got rich whilst doing it.'

Harry stared.

'I mean, why would I ask you if I didn't think you could do it?' said Gaggenow.

'Seems like good plan,' said Barl. 'Return Starheart to overlord and save galaxy from invasion, clear name, get bounty hunters off back.'

'Job done!' said Gaggenow.

'Yeah, but it's doing a deal with you. The biggest fraudster in the galaxy. How do I know I can trust you?' said Harry.

'What choice do you have?'

Gaggenow was right. Harry had to do this before he could go home – really go home. Once it was done, maybe he could even take his mum on some galactic adventures.

Harry sat back and buckled himself in, being careful not to trap his squid finger.

'Dave,' he said, 'charge up the quantum drive.'

HARRY sat in the Captain's Cabin. They were hurtling away from Earth as fast as they could, chased by Squeaker Longstockings, the Vizier, and Clypeus of the Leptira. Werdle had been firing up the quantum drive and any second now they were going to jump into hyperspace and hopefully lose the pursuit. They'd agreed to split up, Gaggenow heading off to the *Greene One*. He was going to go on ahead, try to set something up. They'd agreed to rendezvous at Hub Prime, the capital planet of the galaxy to try to get an audience with the Galactic Overlord, give him the Starheart and clear their names.

In the meantime, Harry decided to check on his account. He sat at the captain's console, calling up his Grand Bank account on the monitor.

Harry logged in and his details came up.

Account holder: Captain Harry Greene
Account Type: Much Revered Super Beloved Customer Premium Account
Account Number: 0783392666/HG
Balance: 0 Galactic Credits

Balance...what? Harry put a hand up to his mouth! Some kind of admin error, surely? Where had all his money gone?

Something flashed at the top of the screen – a private message on...Spacebook? What was that? Harry clicked on it. It took him to the Spacebook page of...The Great Gaggenow, Intergalactic Adventurer and Explorer of Worlds.

Up flashed a little message.

'Oh, come on, Harry. Your mum's first name and your birthday? My left foot could have hacked this account.

Yours richly, Gaggenow the Magnificent.'

' NOOOOOOOOOOOOoooooo!' howled Harry.

ACKNOWLEDGEMENTS

I would like to thank Galacto Burgers for their sponsorship of the writing of this book, not least by keeping me well supplied with Pongo burgers... Well, except for that one burger that they accidentally filled with MikMak mustard. That didn't help. But anyway, mostly it was good.

Also, my pal Dave, who helped me with the plot and stuff. He's actually a computer AI, of course, calling himself Dave Morris. He tries so hard to pass himself off as human but mostly fails. I must also thank my editors, Megan Larkin, Rosie McIntosh and Emily Sharratt for helping to decode these messages from space. And also Jamie Lenman for his most excellent art, so good that Clypeus and the Leptira have promised not to eat him, as long as he keeps up the good work.

Jamie Thomson is from another planet. Well, actually he isn't really, he just looks like he's from another planet. He claims to get messages beamed to him from the stars, sent by Harry himself, who is lost in space. I mean, Harry has a spaceship and a crew and everything. Apparently.

Sounds ridiculous to me, just like this author fellow. Anyway, Jamie also wrote the *Dark Lord* series of books and won the Roald Dahl Funny Prize in 2012. Apparently Harry Greene loved those books, and that's why he chose Jamie to write his story for him.

Jamie has a website if you want to know more about his crazy stories.

www.jamiethomson.com

Read on for a sneak peek at
Jamie Thomson's hilarious

The Fall

'AAAaaaaaaaaaarrrrrrrrrrrgggggggggghhhhhhh!'

His fall seemed to go on forever. It felt like bits of him were being stripped away, as if he was changing into something else as he fell. After a long time his cries of rage and fear faded and he sank into a kind of sleep, all sensation lost, falling silently in an immense void of nothingness for what seemed like an eternity. Then, suddenly

KA-RUNCH!!!!

Pain, so much pain… Then it faded away and he took in a great shuddering gulp of air. He coughed and spat out a glob of black mucus. He watched as the mucus formed a small puddle of shiny black oil. He lay for a while, just breathing.

The ground felt like hard gravel. He could barely move. He couldn't think properly and he felt weak and listless. The sky above was blue, painfully blue.

He hated blue skies and sunlight.

He needed help. He called out for his lieutenant, Dread Gargon, Hewer of Limbs, but his voice caught in his throat. He tried again.

'Gaa… Gargon, to me!' he tried to bellow in his most commanding tones, but it only came out as a little squeak, high-pitched and boyish. Where was the dark, imperious voice that sent forth his Legions of Dread to bloody war and pitiless plunder?

He tried once more, but again it came out as a high-pitched trill. He groaned and tried raising his head, but couldn't. He wondered whether his Helm of the Hosts of Hell had slipped off again – if it wasn't balanced just right it could catch his neck in an uncomfortable pinch.

He reached up, but there was no Helm at all. He couldn't feel any horns either, or knobbly ridges of bone, only what seemed like a brown mop of hair on a rather small head. And his teeth! They didn't feel right either – no tusks or yellowed fangs to inspire terror and dread. Instead his head felt like a little human head, just like the ones he usually kept impaled on those iron spikes over the Gates of

Doom, or the ones that Gargon wore hanging from his belt.

What was going on and where was Gargon?

There was something else as well. Too much harsh sunlight usually fried his undead flesh like an egg in a pan, but he couldn't feel the usual sunfire burns. Not only that, the sky actually seemed rather beautiful. White clouds drifted serenely across the bright blue canopy of the heavens, and birds sang songs of joy in nearby trees. The sun warmed him nicely and a feeling of…hmmm, let's see now, something he hadn't felt in aeons, a sense of… peace came over him! Yes, that was it. A sense of peace. How could that be? He'd spent years trying to perfect a spell to cover the sky in The Black Vapours of Gloom but now the bright blueness didn't seem to bother him.

A wash of pain came over him again. *That's better,* he thought. He didn't want to feel a sense of peace. It just wasn't the sort of thing he should be feeling. After all, he had his reputation to consider…

With a great effort he was able to turn his head a little and take his eyes off the sky. He saw a low building of dull grey stone on his left, squat and unsightly. Excellent. At least someone was making ugly stuff around here. Maybe it was of Orcish design. You could always rely on Orcs to make ugly stuff.

He saw some kind of banner flying over the building. Runes were written on it, in a strange language. To his surprise he realised he could read them. 'Saveco Supermarket' it said. A market. That didn't sound Orcish. Orcs tended to prefer pillaging to shopping. And Saveco – was he the local overlord, perhaps? Lord Saveco, Smiter of Foes, the Pitiless One? Something about it didn't sound right.

He looked the other way. What he saw was even stranger to his eyes. Several rows of oddly shaped metal boxes gleamed in the sunlight. They were of all kinds of different colours, and glass plates had been set into their sides. They rested on four wheels, thickly encrusted with some kind of black resin that looked like the hard-set mucus of the Giant Spiderbeasts of Skorpulos. One of the boxes suddenly shuddered into life, rattling away with a terrible noise like the coughing shriek of the dragon before it discharged its fiery breath.

He tried to bend the box to his will. If it was a thing of evil, it should instinctively follow his command. 'Beast of Steel and Mucus – I command you in the Name of the Dark Lord and by the Power of the Nine Hells!'

But his voice came out as a querulous squeak. The metal box moved away as if he hadn't even spoken. Then he noticed what looked like a human woman inside the box, peering out through the glass panels. Of course! It was some kind of horseless chariot, driven no doubt by magic. The woman must be a potent witch indeed to command such a thing. The wizardry of mortals was getting sophisticated and powerful. He'd have to watch them more closely.

Then he heard a voice – another human by the sound of it – shouting, 'Hey, are you all right, lad?'

Buy these books or endure my eternal wrath!
Yours insincerely, Dirk Lloyd

978 1 40831 511 8 Pbk
978 1 40831 655 9 eBook

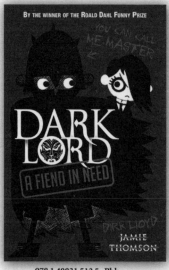

978 1 40831 512 5 Pbk
978 1 40831 656 6 eBook

978 1 40833 025 8 Pbk
978 1 40833 028 9 eBook